A NIGHTMARE'S DOZEN

W9-BSK-322

A NIGHTMARE'S DOZEN

Stories from the Dark

EDITED BY
MICHAEL STEARNS

ILLUSTRATED BY
MICHAEL HUSSAR

LAUREL-LEAF BOOKS

Deepest thanks to Gordon Van Gelder, without whom this book would not have come about.

Published by
Bantam Doubleday Dell Books for Young Readers
a division of
Random House, Inc.
1540 Broadway
New York, New York 10036

The trademark Laurel-Leaf Library® is registered in the U.S. Patent and Trademark Office. The trademark Dell® is registered in the U.S. Patent and Trademark Office.

Visit us on the Web! www.randomhouse.com

Educators and librarians, for a variety of teaching tools, visit us at www.randomhouse.com/teachers

---

ISBN: 0-440-22746-1

RL: 5.9

Reprinted by arrangement with Harcourt Brace & Company

Printed in the United States of America

October 1999

10 9 8 7 6 5 4 3 2 1

OPM

For Thomas Huse,
Lynn Baer, and
Connie Vanlandingham,
with thanks

night•mare's doz•en \ 'nīt-ˌmārz 'dəzən \ *n* [ME fr. *night* + *mare dozeine*] (13c) **1:** any curse-employed number between twelve and fifteen **2** *slang*: number of dreams in a cycle of recurring nightmares **3** *archaic*: number of dark spirits who ride a nightmare (usu. portrayed as a coal black horse) to a dreamer's deathbed

CONTENTS

A BUMP IN THE NIGHT

In less enlightened times, nightmares were believed to be evil spirits that attacked a person in her sleep, perching on her chest till she awoke to find nothing in her room but the dark and her own fear.

Modern thinkers now tell us that nightmares are caused by much more ordinary things: belated shock from some fright during the day, a reaction to a spicy dinner, anxiety over a spelling test. In our nightmares, our brains play out possibilities that our waking minds won't allow. We feel at last the delayed terrors of a close call earlier in the day, or we experience beforehand the fears that accompany some task we dread, or we discover something about ourselves that our waking minds are too cowardly to consider in the nervous light of day. Nightmares are a release valve, a place to make dry runs, a place to fail spectacularly. They are a place to exorcise demons. And all they cost is a little sleep.

It is the same with scary stories. Like bad dreams, they can be release mechanisms.

Some critics think scary stories are bad for readers, that they indulge dark urges and encourage the worst in us. These critics point to the troubles of our times and blame them on the horrors in the stories we tell ourselves.

But scary stories don't work that way.

Instead, they allow us to try on scarier worlds for size, to see if, say, meeting up with that hundred-foot cockroach will really be that bad (it will), or whether it might be better if the dead stayed in their graves (*far* better). And more than that, stories allow us to consider the inconsiderable, the things we can't talk about in polite company. Why *do* the dead haunt us—if not literally, then figuratively? Why is it both a blessing and a curse to "get what you deserve"? We find out in scary stories.

No one likes to admit it, but there is usually a burr of pleasure in our shriek of terror when a character goes to see what's scratching at the door. *He* might get scared to death (or worse), but *we're* safe at home under the covers, knuckles white on our flashlights, real terror just a faraway bump in the night.

A NIGHTMARE'S DOZEN

STEVE RASNIC TEM

THE HIDEAWAY MAN

People were always asking
John how he and Dave could
be friends. After all, they had
nothing in common. John himself admitted that was true.
John liked to be outside as
much as possible, even in snow
and drizzle (which drove his
mom crazy). Dave liked to stay
inside, mostly, and mostly in
his room. John liked all kinds
of movies, even the old black-
and-white ones. Dave had a
hard time sitting through a

movie unless it was a cartoon. John liked girls. Really liked girls. Dave wouldn't even talk in front of a girl.

"Hideaway hideaway Hideaway Man..."

"Shut up, Dave."

Dave grinned down at him from the edge of the bed, the grin in his red face like a knife-cut in a tomato. "Hideaway hideaway Hideaway Man...," Dave repeated, more softly but a whole lot more sarcastically.

That was another thing. Dave was always saying dumb things like that. John was sure he must have said dumb things sometimes, too. All guys said dumb things sometimes. He supposed girls did, too, but if you liked the girl in question he guessed nothing she ever said sounded dumb to you.

But Dave was the champion at saying dumb things. Silly things. Crazy things.

"Hideaway hideaway Hideaway Man..." Grin grin grin.

"Shut *up*, Dave!"

Like this hideaway thing. Every time John stayed over at Dave's house he had to sleep in this little bed Dave's mom called a hideaway bed. It stayed under Dave's bed most of the time, then when Dave had company his mom rolled it out.

As far as John knew he was the only company Dave had ever had. If only Dave weren't such a tomatohead!

Anyway, ever since they were little kids Dave had said the hideaway bed had its own "Hideaway Man" who came and slept in it when no one but Dave was around. "But someday, maybe...," Dave would say, and grin. "Someday, maybe, if you're *real* good..."

Grin grin grin. "Maybe someday you'll get to see the Hideaway Man, too."

"Oh yeah, sure, Dave. Get a life, why don't you?"

And Dave never said anything back. He never would talk about it. He just grinned. That was the scary part.

John didn't know why he kept going over to Dave's house. He was too old for Dave's silliness. Force of habit, he guessed. They'd been spending the night at each other's houses since they were little kids.

No, they didn't have much in common. Everybody said so, even John's mom.

But what John and Dave did have in common was something most of John's other friends didn't know much about. And it was something he wanted to talk about, but he just couldn't. Neither John nor Dave had a dad.

John had lost his dad when he was only about two years old. Well, not lost. His dad died in a car wreck. Sometimes John imagined that his dad was out getting a present for him when he had the wreck, and so it was partly John's fault his dad had died; but that was pretty silly, for sure. He thought that but never told anybody.

That was another difference between Dave and him. Dave was always telling people about every crazy thing that came into his head. Like the Hideaway Man.

John had always felt a little funny about not having a dad. Especially about not remembering him very well and wondering if his dad had been a good person or a bad person and if John were going to turn out to be just like him. His mom and the relatives always told John his dad had been a real good person, but that didn't mean much. People were always saying nice things about dead people.

Still, as much as John thought about his dad, it was like his dad was the most alive person John knew. He wasn't there, but it was like he was there all the time. Pretty silly thinking, John thought, and he knew better than to tell anybody.

Dave's dad wasn't dead, as far as anybody knew; he'd just walked away when Dave was only a few months old. So Dave had even fewer memories of his dad than John had. But Dave talked about his dad more.

"I think he was a pilot. I'm pretty sure Mom told me that one time. He was a fighter pilot and he shot down a lot of enemy planes. And he bombed places, but only military targets. He never killed civilians."

"I thought you said he was a police officer, and he'd had to go undercover and that was why he left you and your mom."

"That was afterward. They won't let you be a pilot forever, you know. You get tired." Then Dave grinned. He always grinned when he was nervous.

What a tomatohead.

Actually, Dave hadn't brought up the Hideaway Man in a long time. Then tonight he'd been going on and on about his dad being a CIA agent, at least when he wasn't being a genius scientist, or a movie star, or an athlete, or something. That's what had started it. John had wanted to talk about girls and Dave had gone on and on with these crazy lies about his dad, his face getting redder and redder, grinning like an idiot, until

4

finally John got mad. He just couldn't take it anymore.

"Dave, your dad walked out on you and your mom because he didn't want the hassle. I've heard your mom tell my mom that. Come on! I've heard her tell you that, too. He wasn't brave, he was a coward. He ran away from being a father. And I guess he drank a lot, didn't he? Your mom said he used to hit her. He hit you, too, she said."

Well, he was sorry as soon as he said it. The way Dave looked at him, as if he couldn't believe John could be this mean to him. John couldn't believe it, either. He felt terrible.

"Hideaway hideaway Hideaway Man." Grin grin grin. Dave leaned down from the edge of his bed, looking like a crazy person. John figured his old friend would keep this up all night now, but he guessed he deserved it. He never should have said anything about Dave's dad. He would have been really upset if somebody said something about his own dad. He looked up from the hideaway bed into Dave's enormous, grinning tomatohead.

John felt terrible, but he tried not to say anything more. Just "I'm going to bed now, Dave." Then he turned over and tried to go to sleep.

But he could still feel Dave grinning at him.

In the middle of the night John got up to go to the bathroom. Dave was asleep, facing the wall. When John got back Dave wasn't in his bed, but there was someone under the covers of the hideaway bed.

"Come on, Dave, get out of my bed. I need my sleep. We *both* need our sleep."

Dave didn't make any sound.

"Dave, come on..." John reached down and pulled back the covers.

A man in a dark suit rolled over and looked up at John. But the man didn't really look. The man had no face, just a big black shadow where his face should have been.

The man with no face reached out for John, and John turned and ran.

He ran out of the bedroom and down the hall and down the steps, where he stumbled and fell. He groaned and rubbed his face. Then a pale hand came out of the darkness and touched his shoulder.

"John." It was Dave, his face glowing a warm pink in the dark.

"Dave? Dave, was that your dad?"

Dave leaned over, his face turning redder. "I thought it was *your* dad." And then he grinned and grinned and grinned. "Hideaway hideaway Hideaway Man!"

"Cut it *out*, Dave!"

"No, no. I *mean* it," Dave said. "I think that's your dad."

John stared at Dave, wondering what a crazy person looked like—if a crazy person looked like Dave; because what Dave was saying was *real* crazy. "My dad is dead," John said. "You *know* that."

"Just tell me what color hair your dad had," Dave said.

John hesitated. As many times as he'd looked at his dad's pictures, for a second he couldn't remember what his dad's hair color had been. "Blond," he finally said. "But a little darker, I guess. Maybe a real light brown."

"Go look, then. Go look in the hideaway bed."

John didn't say anything. He looked up the steps. There appeared to be a dim light on at the end of the hall, where Dave's bedroom was. Going back up there was the absolutely last thing he wanted to do, so why was he walking toward the steps, walking up those steps to the upstairs hall and Dave's room? Like some dumb character in a movie going right toward the danger even though you're yelling at him—in your head, at least—to stay away.

But now John knew why those dumb characters do that. They just *have* to know. He guessed we're all just tomatoheads that way.

When he got to Dave's bedroom door he found that it was open. He eased his head around and looked into the room. The dark man, the Hideaway Man, had lain back down on the hideaway bed, with his face that was no face turned away from the door. The man's hair was light colored. It could have been blond or a real light brown. Or it could have been gray. It could have been white.

"That can't be my dad," John whispered. "My dad is dead." But Dave didn't say anything, and when John turned around he saw that Dave wasn't there.

It's bedtime, a low voice rumbled from the room, rumbled from the hideaway bed. *Little boys should be asleep.*

And just like in the movies, or just like in a dream, John discovered that he could not move, could not move an inch, even though he was terrified and wanted to run away as fast as he could—run down the stairs and out the door and all the way home to his mother and his own safe bed. He wanted to start screaming, start yelling for Dave's mother to wake up and come out of her room and help; but he couldn't do that, either.

John could hear the Hideaway Man get up out of bed and stumble across the room behind him. And still John could not move. He could *smell* the man behind him, and the man smelled like he'd been drinking—and John knew hardly any drinkers, so he couldn't understand where he knew that smell from. Dave's father used to drink.

"Dave! It's your dad!" John screamed, as he started to run. But the Hideaway Man grabbed him and wrapped his arms around him, arms that seemed way too long, arms that were more like two snakes wrapping around him, arms that squeezed and squeezed until John could hardly breathe.

But the kind of funny thing, the really strange thing, was that John also felt like he didn't *want* the Hideaway Man to let go, that he actually *liked* the Hideaway Man squeezing him, hugging him.

"I *hate* you, I *hate* you!" Dave's voice exploded inside the room, as powerful as the Hideaway Man's smell.

The Hideaway Man let go of John, and John stepped back, and there was Dave holding his baseball bat, swinging it and beating the Hideaway Man with it as hard as he could. "I hate...you...I...hate you..." Dave gasped, almost out of breath, as the bat passed through the Hideaway Man's body and the Hideaway Man started to fall apart, pieces of him disappearing, an arm and then a leg...but on the face that was no face there was a grin grin grin just like Dave's, just like a tomatohead with a knife smile cut into it.

"I *hate* you! I *hate* you!" John joined in, kicking and swinging his fists into the Hideaway Man's disappearing body. And it was true, John *did* hate him, because suddenly John remembered something he'd always known, something he'd heard his mom tell his uncle that he wasn't supposed to hear.

John's dad had been a drinker, too. That was why he'd had the accident. John's dad hadn't been going to get John a present. John's dad had been coming back from a bar when he ran his car off the road.

"Hideaway hideaway Hideaway Man," Dave whispered to the old empty clothes lying on the floor at their feet. But Dave did not grin this time.

And then John knew why he and Dave had been friends for so long. Because they had so much in common.

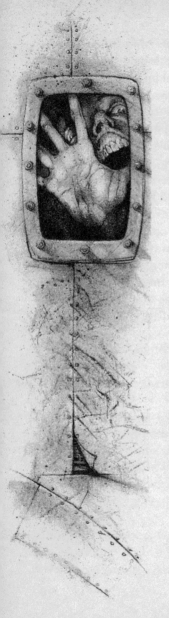

M A R T H A   S O U K U P

ALITA IN THE AIR

A loud voice over the speakers
said they were descending into
Tucson. Alita's ears started
hurting. Sick with boredom, really quite sure you could throw
up from boredom—that would
be what the airsick bags were
for—she tried to see if there
were anything interesting out
the airplane's window.

No, there wasn't.

And she thought about
landing and all the bother and
nonsense and Uncle Roy who

was really boring too. Uncle Roy and the horrible forsaken desert and all of the summer there. And she thought of something mischievous to do when she got there.

But she didn't think she'd do it, really.

The plane landed with a bump and a jostle, pushing her head forward as they dragged to a halt down the runway. The seat belt sign turned off with a *ping* after the plane had driven around for a while, by which time Alita had already unfastened her buckle. She stood up on her seat, her head hunched under the overhead baggage compartments, impatient for all the well-fed grown-up bodies to get out of her way in the narrow aisle.

"Alita?" said the flight attendant, in the syrupy voice she hated. He was the one who had taken her from the check-in guy in Chicago and held her hand like she was a baby, all the way down the aisle to her seat in the back. He was the one who'd pinned the plastic airline wings over the picture of the Ferris wheel on her T-shirt, next to the sticker that said UNACCOMPANIED CHILD. The tag on his uniform said JERRY, and she didn't like him any better than she liked anyone else.

"We'll just be waiting for the other passengers to leave the plane. Then I'll take you up to meet your uncle," Jerry said sweetly. Alita nodded and fingered the plastic souvenir pin and hated Arizona. Just looking out the window at the low airport buildings shimmering in the sun made her hate it.

Arizona was so bad it was worse than being on a stupid airplane, she was sure. At least on an airplane they mostly left you alone. Uncle Roy had been on the

11

phone with her mother for an *hour,* and all the plans they'd made for her next month were disgusting.

"Okay time to go," Jerry said, like it was one word. He put his hand out. Alita looked away from it. He grabbed her hand and genially hustled her down the plane's aisle. "So you're vacationing in Tucson? That's just great. What are you going to do?"

"Nothing," Alita said.

"That's just great," Jerry said, dragging her down the aisle and into the jetway that connected the plane to the airport building.

Great, Alita thought. *Just great.* There was a blast of hot air where the jetway joined to the building; it made her shiver. *Great.* The building was air-conditioned, but surrounded by Arizona. Uncle Roy would probably want to go right out iguana hunting, or whatever they did in Arizona.

"I have Alita here," Jerry said to the woman at the check-in podium. He handed her the papers Alita's mother had given to the man at the podium in Chicago.

The podium woman's name tag said CHARLOTTE. "Well let's see who we've got here," Charlotte said, smiling, in the same syrupy one-word rush Jerry talked in. Alita scowled. A man came forward from the crowd, bald, and smiling, too.

"Hi, Alita!" said Uncle Roy. He was holding a pink teddy bear, for cripe's sake.

So she did it, the mischief she had thought of on the airplane.

"Who are *you?*" she said to Uncle Roy.

"What?" said Uncle Roy.

"What?" said Charlotte, her dumb talk-to-the-kid

12

smile fading. "Honey, isn't this the person who's supposed to meet you?"

"I've never seen him," Alita said. She raised her voice. "My uncle Roy is supposed to meet me."

"I'm Roy Mahaffey," Uncle Roy said.

"Isn't this your uncle Roy?" Charlotte said; and, "Uncle Roy has black hair and he's taller," said Alita, at the same time. This could work. She fingered the stupid UNACCOMPANIED CHILD sticker and widened her eyes to look like a very kidnappable kid.

"Alita, you remember me," Uncle Roy said.

"I want my uncle Roy," Alita said.

"Sir, could I see some ID?" Charlotte said.

"This is crazy," said Uncle Roy, digging in his pocket.

"I want my uncle Roy!" Alita said. She wondered if she were playing it too hard. But grown-up strangers never did seem to know the difference between a twelve-year-old and a kid of five or six.

"It's the right address. Sir, what's your phone number?" Charlotte was peering at Uncle Roy's driver's license and at the forms that Jerry had brought from the plane with Alita.

"Look, even on the driver's license he doesn't have black hair like my uncle Roy! It's a fake!" Alita said.

"What's wrong with you?" Uncle Roy said, reaching out to touch her arm.

Alita shrieked and jumped behind Charlotte. Uncle Roy looked baffled. Alita grabbed Charlotte's sleeve. She had to stretch her eyes wide to keep from laughing.

Charlotte shuffled some papers and called a supervisor and for a while there were a lot of people standing around, and finally the supervisor told Uncle Roy that if he left they wouldn't call the police.

"But I never had black hair, and you know who I am! I bought you that book for Christmas," he said to Alita. Alita made a show of looking away from him. It had been a stupid book anyway.

Uncle Roy walked away slowly, hunching his shoulders, the pink teddy bear dangling in his loose grip.

"Now what?" Alita asked Charlotte. She was feeling cheerful. The first part of it had been kind of embarrassing, lying such a big lie; but once she'd gotten used to it, it was exciting, making the grown-ups jump. Anyway, Uncle Roy wasn't even in trouble. He'd left before anyone called the police.

"Now," said Charlotte. She pressed her lips together, which made her look less like an airline person and more like Alita's mother when she was tired and angry. Which was how Alita's mother looked most of the time lately.

"Now we'll put her back on a plane home," said Charlotte's supervisor, who was so important he didn't have a name on a tag. "And since this one is turning around in another forty minutes, we should get her back on it now. Call an attendant."

The supervisor wrote on a lot of papers and gave them to the new flight attendant, whose name tag said MIMI. Mimi smiled briefly at Alita and hauled her by the hand back into the jetway. The hot air blasted them again where the jetway attached, and Alita felt very clever to have avoided the whole trauma of a summer in the desert.

On the way back, Alita watched the sky turn red

14

and purple with sunset until it was mostly black, then pulled down the plastic window shade.

The flight attendant gave her a headset for free, which was good because the one she'd paid for on the way to Arizona had taken a big chunk of her pocket money. They were showing another movie her mother wouldn't let her see in a movie theater, although when the lady started to take her shirt off in the man's living room, the scene changed quickly to a police station.

It was a boring movie, on a little television screen hanging from the ceiling, partly blocked by a passenger's bald head. Just as Alita was getting sick of it, dinner was served, something with noodles that stuck to the plastic tray and a measly cookie for dessert. Alita finished eating the cookie, took off the headphones, and played Game Boy.

About the time she reached level 17 of Rajah Princess, she started to think about what she could say to her mother when she landed.

"Uncle Roy wasn't there," she'd say. *He was there, Alita,* she imagined her mother saying. "No, no, no! A kidnapper pretending to be Uncle Roy was there." In her mind, Alita's mother shook her head angrily. *Haven't you heard of the telephone, Alita? Uncle Roy called me and told me all about it.*

Alita swallowed. "It didn't look like Uncle Roy," she told her mother in her head; and, "Actually, nobody showed up at all—Uncle Roy must have been telling you a story so he wouldn't get in trouble"; and, "He told me he was a kidnapper!" In her mind, her mother frowned harder and harder.

The plane landed before she could think of anything

that wouldn't make her mother frown. "Okay time to go," Mimi said, like it was one word, and clamped a hand around Alita's wrist and pulled her out into the jetway to the O'Hare Airport building. The air that came through there was pretty hot, too, and muggy. "They called your mother from Tucson, so she should be here." She delivered Alita to the podium, smiled brightly, and left.

When Alita saw her mother, standing there with Marsh-mouth at her hip and frowning just like Alita had imagined, she could only think of one thing to say.

"That's not my mother," she whispered to the man at the podium, ALFRED.

"What?" said Alfred; and, "Alita Matilda Anderson!" said her mother.

Alfred looked at Alita.

Nothing for it: "That proves it's not my mother," Alita said. "She guessed my middle name wrong."

Her mother was frowning very hard.

"Matilda Brunhilda what a pill-da," said Marsh.

"It's not Matilda, it's—" She got on tiptoes and whispered into Alfred's ear. "Mimi," she whispered. "See if she can guess that!"

Alfred pursed his lips and looked through all the papers. "It just says Alita M. Anderson here," he said.

"I know my own name," Alita said. "The international *kidnapping* conspiracy doesn't."

"What's the child's middle name?" Alfred asked her mother.

"Also, I don't live here," she whispered to Alfred. "My dad lives in California, but he's moving to New York, and he sent me to Chicago to visit my grandma while we move. Does she look old enough to be my grandma?"

"Middle name?" Alfred repeated.

"Oh, for Pete's— Young lady, when I get you home!" Alita's mother said.

Alita cried, "Don't let her steal me!"

"Can you tell me the name?" Alfred said.

"I never—it's Matilda. After her great-grandmother."

Alita had always hated that name. "No," she said.

"I'm not going to play this game," her mother said. She looked at Alfred and he looked at her. She turned red.

"Myrtle," she said. "Meredith. Megan. Margerie. Mehitabel. For Pete's sake!"

"I don't know this stupid girl, either," Marsh said. Alita glared at him, changed her mind, and smiled sweetly. Imagine not having to share with Marsh-mouth anymore. Marsh had on his most innocent face, the one he used to tell their mother whoppers about Alita.

"She said she was going to get another kid because I didn't scrub the floors fast enough," Marsh said loudly.

"Young man!" their mother said. Her voice was as loud as pots and pans smashing against a wall. Alita had seen her angry hundreds of times since Alita's father had moved away to wherever he'd really gone— no one had ever told her where—but this was the most ever. The plan had better work, or she was sure to be cooked.

"And do the laundry and peel the vegetables and mow the lawn and wax the car and—"

17

"Don't let her take me for child labor!" Alita said. Marsh was pretty clever, really, for a stupid kid.

Then Alfred called his supervisor, and there was a lot of fuss and noise and Alita was the center of everyone's attention again. Alita's mother turned redder and redder yet. Finally she picked Marsh right up off the floor—his canvas sneakers kicking ten inches in the air—and said, "Make your bed and lie in it, young lady," and turned on her heel. Alita watched them leave, Marsh dangling in their mother's grip but not forgetting to stick his tongue out at her good-bye.

Victory! By the time she decided to come home, her mother would be sorry.

"Now what?" she said cheerfully to Alfred and his supervisor and all the grown-ups crowded around.

They looked at each other.

"There's a red-eye flight to Portland, Oregon," Alfred said. Alita blinked in surprise, but thought she shouldn't argue.

He typed a lot on his computer and the supervisor filled out some forms and Alita got put on a cart that whizzed her across the airport to a different terminal, where RAMON took her by the wrist and hustled her onto another airplane. There were very few people on it, mostly businessmen sleeping with their jackets laid out, like blankets with arms, across their chests.

Alita was sort of hungry, but all Ramon gave out to eat was pretzels, so she drank a lot of cola and stayed up all night. No one cared if she went to sleep. That was fun for a while, but the plane didn't have a movie and there was no rap on the music channels and the left earpiece on the earphones didn't make any sound.

Still, she could play Game Boy way past anyone's bedtime.

Rajah Princess wasn't as hard in the little-screen version, and she didn't have her other cartridges. They were in her purse. Her purse was gone. She pushed the call button for Ramon and told him. He shrugged. "It's probably in Chicago," he said, hurrying off to answer another call.

The sun was coming up when they landed in Portland. Ramon pulled her down the aisle to the terminal building, where SYDNEY looked at her papers and put her on a plane to San Diego. Alita was very tired, but a baby was crying in the seat behind her, and she couldn't sleep. She asked the flight attendant, MARY-SUE, if she could move seats. "The plane is full," Mary-Sue told her shortly, and handed her a cold mushroom omelette. An hour and a half later, Mary-Sue grabbed Alita's hand and hustled her out to meet BOB at the podium.

Bob wrote some things on her papers and sent her to the gate right next door. Alita's stomach hurt and her eyes felt like they were full of sand. It was hard to shut them and hard to keep them open.

She nearly fell asleep in an airport chair anyway, but then WENDY had her wrist in an iron grip and was dragging her off. Wendy plopped Alita down in a seat between a fat businessman and a fat guy in a baseball hat and a smelly T-shirt. They both ordered a lot of drinks and told loud awful jokes to each other over Alita's head the whole way to Newark. Alita got out her Game Boy and tried to ignore them.

The battery died just about the time the pilot told

everyone over the speakers that they were crossing the Mississippi. Alita groaned. She put the blanket over her head and tried to sleep. Maybe she slept, but if she did, she dreamed the guffaws of two large men all the way through it.

"Not another one of these," said PAT in Newark. He tapped on his computer and wrote some things on the papers and sent Alita right back on the same airplane, this time with GEOFFREY.

"Can I get some batteries somewhere?" Alita asked Geoffrey.

"We don't keep batteries on the airplane," Geoffrey said. He gave her a pack of playing cards with pictures of vodka bottles and the airline's name on them.

No good solitaire game fit on a little airplane tray.

Alita flew to Minneapolis, and San Francisco, and Houston, and Jacksonville. It was probably on the Houston flight that she misplaced the dead Game Boy. From Jacksonville she took a bunch of little hops up the East Coast to Boston. By Boston her hair felt really greasy, and there were stains on her T-shirt.

"I want to go home now," she told BERENICE.

"Home would be California, or would it be New York?" said Berenice, peering at her papers through glasses that had a chain behind them. "No, wait: Tucson?"

"Aurora, Illinois," Alita said, trying to comb her hair smooth with her fingers. Her brush had been in her purse.

"Portland?" said Berenice.

"It's near Chicago," Alita said.

"I don't have any record of that," said Berenice. "We'll put you on a plane to Boise."

"Can I have a bath?" Alita said. She was exhausted.

Berenice handed her off to JOE, who put her on a seat near the bathroom, which had a long line to it as soon as the seat belt sign went off. Finally Alita went in and tried to wash her hair in the tiny little sink, using liquid soap from the pump. She got water all over her T-shirt. The ink ran on the UNACCOMPANIED CHILD sticker.

Joe *tsk*'d and got her another sticker. "We have to follow procedure," he said.

"I want to go home now," Alita said. Joe handed her a bag of sugar-coated peanuts and didn't stop by her seat for the rest of the flight.

She flew to Seattle and Fresno and Las Vegas and Atlanta. She ripped her T-shirt in Atlanta and HOLLY gave her a new one with the airline's logo on it. It was too big even to be baggy. It might as well have been a nightgown.

She tried to use the airplane phone to call her mother. The phone needed a credit card to work. She tried to get to an airport phone, but MICHELLE held on to her wrist at the gate in Saint Louis, and RANDY kept his hand clamped on her shoulder in Cleveland, and JOHN made her sit in an airport chair and didn't take his eyes off her until they were ready to board in El Paso.

When they did announce it was time to preboard unaccompanied minors in El Paso, Alita made a break for the phone banks. John was much faster than she was, and she was hustled onto the plane before she had a chance to protest.

And after that, they kept her on the plane after everyone else had disembarked. If the plane was going on to somewhere else, she stayed in her seat. If it wasn't, she sat on the plane watching the cleaning people put the magazines back into the magazine bin and throw out people's crumpled tissues, until another plane was ready and KATHERINE or PHIL or GREGORY escorted her to it.

But she never was on the ground very much. Most of the time she was high above the earth, flying through clouds and sunshine and rain and peering down, in the middle of the night, at the thousands of tiny lights that were each someone's home, snug and firm on the ground.

She never seemed to be able to sleep.

She was always too cold.

The airplane food was awful.

The seats were lumpy, and the other seats pressed in so close all around her it felt hard to breathe.

On long flights, she would slip her seat belt off when the FASTEN SEAT BELTS sign went off, and stand in the tiny galley at the back of the airplane by the bathrooms. That was the nearest thing to breathing space on an airplane, but you couldn't be there more than a minute or two without being in someone's way. Passengers would jostle past her on their way to one of the bathrooms.

"Excuse me," Alita said until the words came out automatically without her thinking about them. Sometimes the passenger was a kid, who'd look at her curiously and try to strike up a conversation about where she was flying to. For a while she avoided kids; then for a while she told whoppers about the trip to Paris or India she'd just come from or was on now; and then it made her sick to have to talk about where she could be instead of on an airplane, and she avoided kids again.

The flight attendants were always moving, rushing around the narrow spaces of the airplane, doing everything. When they weren't moving Alita from one plane to another, they paid no attention to her, so she could squeeze herself into a corner—never out of the way for very long, someone always needed something from wherever you could stow yourself—and watch them and listen. The flight attendants smiled at passengers and sighed when the passengers' backs were turned. They pushed stray hair back behind their ears, took deep breaths, and hurried off to answer calls. When they thought no one was looking, they leaned heavily on the steel galley countertop with their eyes shut. Just for a moment: then they would put on bright expressions again and pour someone some orange juice. Alita, part of the airplane furniture, saw things the passengers didn't, and kept them to herself.

One night, on a red-eye from Detroit to Oakland, LILLIAN leaned over her and tucked the thin airline blanket up under Alita's chin. It was the nicest thing anyone had done in a very long time. Alita whispered, her eyes hot and squeezed shut, "Can't I go home?"

The woman murmured, so softly Alita could barely hear her, "What home?" Alita kept her eyes shut and strained to hear over the rush of the airplane's jets. "Look out the window: a million little lights. A million

23

little houses. Do you belong to any of them? Do any of them know where you are?"

"But I have to belong somewhere," Alita whispered.

"You owe two hundred thousand dollars in airfare. More each flight. Where do you think you belong now?"

Alita shuddered and opened her eyes. Lillian was three rows ahead, pouring a drink for a skinny woman in a pink suit. The flight attendant's face was a polite blank, but when she turned and glanced at Alita there was exhausted sympathy on her face.

Alita shut her eyes again and slept fitfully. She dreamed a half-awake dream of the airplane flying thousands and thousands and thousands of miles away from Earth, until Earth was a twinkling little light out the window indistinguishable from all the others. When she opened her eyes and looked outside, she was confused about whether she was looking down at distant houses or distant planets.

Her hurting ears let her know they were descending into Oakland. After the grown-ups and their Accompanied Children had all filed off the plane, Alita stood up, feeling stiff and sore all over. The cleaning crew was getting on the plane.

Without a word, Alita took a trash bag from one of the women and started to pick up little pieces of paper and junk the passengers had dropped on the floor.

Lillian stood by the door to the jetway, talking to the pilot. When Alita caught her eye, Lillian smiled and nodded, and the pilot did, too.

They finished cleaning the plane, the cleaning crew and Alita, and Lillian took Alita's wrist and hustled her out, saying, "You have a nice time, okay?" like any flight attendant, and handed her off to SOPHIE, who put Alita on a plane to Dallas–Fort Worth.

Many months later Alita landed in Chicago, and after she'd cleaned the plane and helped with the baggage and was being taken to a gate for Boise, she looked and looked for her mother or even Marsh, but all the smiling faces belonged to strangers.

Now she looked forward to landings. When the passengers were gone, she could vacuum and change toilet-paper rolls and do something besides pretend to be a passenger herself. She wasn't a passenger.

One day, when she had worn out another airline T-shirt and her jeans were too snug around the hips, PATRICIA and JO gave her, instead of another shirt and pants, a wheeled carry-on suitcase like the ones the flight attendants all used. Alita looked at it and looked at them; they looked silently back at her. She unzipped the case. Inside it was a navy blue skirted suit and a striped blouse, identical to theirs.

Wordlessly, she took them into the bathroom. There, with the efficiency she'd learned from a thousand hours in that minute space, she stripped off her old life—the worn-out kid's T-shirt and jeans—stuffed it all in the little trash chute, and put on her new one.

A hundred flights later, an UNACCOMPANIED CHILD of thirteen or so named Marshall, half a foot taller than the last time she'd seen him but still shorter than the young woman she was, got on the airplane in Chicago.

"So you're going to have a summer vacation in Tucson how nice," ALITA said in one sugary practiced breath as she pulled him by the wrist through the jetway; and, "You have a nice time okay now?" she said a few hours later, as she left him with the gate attendant.

And when he turned and looked at her, frowning a little, she smiled a perfect flight attendant's smile and said, "And behave yourself."

Then Alita went back home onto the airplane.

LAWRENCE WATT-EVANS

WHAT THE CAT DRAGGED IN

Amber looked up from her book. She could hear Charlie scratching at the front door, wanting to be let in. He wasn't meowing, though, and that usually meant he had something in his mouth.

She looked around, but no one else was in sight; she supposed her parents were both still out, and her brother was off in some other part of the house or yard, out of earshot.

She sighed, then closed the

book and got up out of her chair. She'd been all comfortably curled up with a self-indulgent snack and the newest Xanth novel, and much as she loved him she didn't want to get up just to let Charlie in. If he'd caught something he wasn't supposed to, though, like a squirrel, it might still be alive and she might be able to make him let it go before it was too badly hurt.

And if it were already dead, or if it were something he was *supposed* to catch, like a snake or a rat, it would probably still be a good idea to get it away from him before he got bloodstains on the welcome mat. She left the book on the coffee table and hurried to the door, then paused, holding the knob.

Charlie was still scratching, but not very enthusiastically, and she could hear squeaking and a sort of fluttering noise—had Charlie caught a *bird?* She hadn't realized he was fast enough. She felt a guilty pride at the idea that good ol' Charlie had managed to catch a live bird.

But of course, the bird might have been sick, or it might be just a baby—if it were really a bird at all.

Whatever he'd caught was still alive, and she didn't want it loose in the house; she knelt by the door, one hand ready to fend Charlie or his unknown prey off, and started to turn the knob with the other.

"Hey, Amber," Jason said from behind her, "whatcha doin'?"

Startled, she sat down heavily and turned her head to glare at her kid brother, who had just come down the stairs to find her crouching in the foyer.

"Charlie's caught something," she said. "I want to

get it away from him without letting them in the house."

"Can I help?"

Amber considered that, then nodded.

"I'll wait here," she said, arranging herself on her knees, hands held before her ready to ward off Charlie. "You open the door."

"Got it." Jason stepped up beside her, turned the knob, and opened the door.

Charlie lunged for the interior in a flash of sleek black fur, but Amber was ready for him; she got both arms around him and picked him up, holding him against her shoulder.

Sure enough, there was something in his mouth, something with wings, something that was squirming frantically and squeaking like a frightened guinea pig.

It wasn't a guinea pig, though, and despite the wings it wasn't a bird, either.

Amber didn't get a good look at it; she was too busy keeping Charlie still, and his head was up over her left shoulder, his captive dangling down her back.

She did see the fluttering wings as it went by, though—*transparent* wings. Birds didn't have wings like that, bugs did. And not the nice bugs like butterflies. A dragonfly, maybe?

It was too *big* for a bug, though, wasn't it? Even a dragonfly? And Charlie never bothered bringing bugs into the house; he just ate them out on the lawn.

And bugs didn't *squeal;* the thing was still squeaking, whatever it was.

"Jason," she called, "what's he got? I can't see it."

Jason moved around behind her and stared.

He didn't answer at once, and she was too busy with the struggling cat to have much patience. "Come on, Jason, what's Charlie holding?" she demanded.

"Jesus," Jason said.

Amber turned and looked up at her brother. He wasn't supposed to talk like that; he was only ten. "What *is* it?"

"Ol' Charlie's caught a fairy," Jason said.

"What?"

"He's caught a fairy! With wings an' everything!"

"Oh, come on, Jase..."

"No, really! I swear! I'll hold the cat, you look for yourself!" He reached over and grabbed Charlie by the scruff of his neck.

"Not so rough," Amber said. Charlie couldn't help being a hunter; that was just in a cat's nature—it didn't justify Jason hurting him.

The cat growled angrily but couldn't do much more than that. Amber slipped out from under, so that Jason was holding the cat in midair; then she turned and looked.

Jason hadn't been kidding. It *was* a fairy.

"Wow," Amber breathed.

Then she snatched Charlie away from her brother and started swatting the cat on the back. "Let go!" she shouted. "Drop it, cat!"

A real, live fairy *was* a reason to get rough. With a yowl of protest, Charlie released his prey.

The creature fluttered, trying to fly away, but instead fell to the tile floor.

"Get a box," Amber ordered Jason. She looked at

30

the fairy, then quickly opened the door, tossed the cat out onto the porch, and then slammed the door shut again.

Jason was back with a shoe box in seconds.

"We need a towel or something, too," Amber said. "To line the box. Something soft, like cotton or something."

"*You* get it," Jason said.

"Okay, but don't touch anything!" Amber dashed away, box in hand, and found one of the fluffy white guest towels on the top shelf in the linen closet. That would do.

A moment later the two children knelt on either side of the wounded fairy, staring down at it.

Except for the wings, it was shaped exactly like a tiny woman—a very thin woman, but a woman. She wore a sort of over-one-shoulder robe that appeared to be made out of tent-caterpillar webbing, but that did little to hide her female figure. Her hair was blond and incredibly fine, drifting out in a halo not just about her head but about most of her body—Amber judged that if the fairy stood up, her hair would reach to her ankles. From the crown of her head to the tips of her tiny pointed toes she measured no more than three or four inches.

And she had wings. Iridescent, glittering, transparent wings that grew from her back, reaching down to her knees and well above her head, and with a wingspan of perhaps six inches.

Her left wing was broken; Charlie's fangs had punched neat holes right through it, holes that were leaking thin clear fluid, and there was a fold to the wing that shouldn't have been there. The almost invisible veins and ribs that gave the wing its strength had been bent until they broke.

The fairy had stopped squeaking and fluttering; she was lying still and staring up at the children.

Cautiously, moving very slowly, Amber reached down and slid a hand under the fairy's undamaged right wing, then used her other hand to push the creature's body onto the fingers. Then she quickly lifted the fairy up and placed it gently in the towel-lined box.

"I'll get some paper towels," Jason said, heading for the kitchen.

Amber looked up, startled, then down at the tiles, at the smear of fluid the fairy had left. She made a face. Then she looked down at the fairy again.

The creature was still staring silently up at her.

"Are you okay?" Amber asked.

Hesitantly, the fairy nodded.

That meant she understood English, Amber realized. Somehow, despite all the stories, despite the thing's almost human appearance, Amber had been thinking of her as an animal.

"Can you talk?" she asked.

"Yes," the tiny thing squeaked.

"Oh, wow," Amber said in a hushed voice.

Jason returned, a wad of paper towels in his hand, and began scrubbing at the smear on the tiles.

"It talks," Amber told him.

Jason looked up at her, startled.

"Go ahead, ask it," Amber said.

Jason looked suspiciously at his sister, then at the creature in the shoe box. "Do you talk?" he demanded.

The fairy nodded.

"A nod isn't talking," Jason told Amber.

"I can speak," the fairy said, before Amber could reply. Her voice was high and squeaky, but very clear and somehow rich.

"I'm sorry the cat got you," Amber said. "And I'm sorry you're hurt. Is there anything we can do to help?"

"Take me home," the fairy answered.

Amber and Jason glanced at one another, then looked back at the fairy.

"How?" Amber said.

"Where?" Jason asked.

"Down behind the garden," the fairy told them.

"What, you mean just in the backyard?" Jason asked.

The fairy nodded.

"I thought it'd be, you know, over the hills and far away, or something," Amber said.

"Behind the garden," the fairy repeated.

Amber and Jason looked at each other; then Amber picked up the shoe box.

"Come on," she said.

Together the two of them went out the front door and around the house, past the sunporch and the patio, down across the wide back lawn, where a rusty croquet wicket still stood even though the slope was far too steep to allow a decent game, to the big old garden where their mother maintained a few patches of herbs and vegetables and a simple floral border while allowing the brick walks and three-fourths of the old beds to be overgrown with weeds.

Charlie meowed at them from under the back porch

as they passed, and Amber told him, "Hush up." She looked down into the box and saw the fairy trembling, and assured her, "Don't worry, we won't let him near you."

At the entrance to the garden, where a white picket gate had once hung but had eventually rotted out and been removed, Amber stopped.

"Now where?" she said. She leaned down to hear the fairy's answer over the buzzing of insects and the rustling of leaves.

"Past the summerhouse," the fairy said.

Jason looked around, puzzled. "You mean the gazebo?" he asked.

The fairy nodded.

Jason and Amber looked at each other. The gazebo at the back of the garden, like the gate, had long since rotted; and two years before, their father had finally torn it down and hauled away the wreckage.

"There's as much fungus and bugs here as wood," he'd said as he loaded the fragments into heavy-duty trash bags. Amber and Jason had watched him work, and they had helped where they could, and neither of them had ever glimpsed any fairies.

Amber shrugged. "Come on," she said.

Together, the pair walked down through the garden, pushing aside weeds that overhung the path. A seedpod burst and Jason sneezed as the powdery fluff reached his nose; a thorn scratched Amber's leg and snagged her sock. At last, though, they reached the site where the gazebo had stood, a wide patch of rich black dirt now thick with green vines and weeds.

They had never played back here much; they hadn't

been allowed in the gazebo, as their parents had said it wasn't safe, and there were plenty of other places that weren't so overgrown. The yard was very big—too big for their parents to maintain properly, especially since it had been left to run wild for years before the family bought the old house at auction.

"Now where?" Amber asked again.

The fairy hauled herself up to peer over the side of the shoe box.

"Straight ahead three steps," she said, "then turn full circle."

Amber blinked. *That* didn't make any sense. She glanced at Jason, who shrugged.

Together they walked forward, Amber counting the steps aloud.

Three steps brought them right up against the towering untrimmed hedge across the back of the garden. Amber could see nothing but hedge.

Feeling foolish, she spun around on her toes—and found herself facing a gap in the hedge.

Astonished, she turned and looked back, and saw the rest of the world unchanged—the half-wild garden, their familiar old house at the top of the slope, Charlie watching from under the back porch.

But there was a gap in the hedge that hadn't been there a moment before.

Jason had turned around as well, and was just as surprised, but trying not to show it. "Come on," he said, stepping into the opening.

Amber followed, the shoe box in her hand, and found herself in a sort of leafy green dome, surrounded on all sides by hedge, sunlight trickling through in drops and speckles. The earth beneath her feet was hard-packed bare black dirt, as if trampled—but who could have trampled it, here in her own backyard?

"Put me down," the fairy said.

Uneasily, Amber lowered the shoe box to the ground.

A breeze rustled the leaves of the hedge, and Amber had a sudden sensation of being watched, as if a thousand tiny eyes were staring at her; she looked quickly around and thought she saw shapes flitting through the hedge.

Leaves turning in the wind? Sunlight scattered by the leaves?

Or other fairies?

"Thank you," the fairy said. "You saved my life. I owe you a boon."

"You're welcome," Amber said automatically. "Listen, you don't owe us anything; we just want you to be safe. Will you be all right here? I mean..."

"What *is* this place?" Jason demanded.

"This is our home," the fairy answered.

"There are others?" Amber asked.

"Oh yes," the fairy replied. "We've been here all along, ever since the garden was first laid out."

"Why don't they show themselves?"

"They don't know you."

"I'd like to see them," Amber said.

"Is that the boon you would ask?"

" 'Boon'?" Amber had to think what the strange word meant; she'd seen it in stories, never heard it spoken before this. "You mean, like a reward? Three wishes, or something?" She would never have believed in wishes ordinarily, but she was talking to a *fairy*, for heaven's sake.

"Our power's not enough in these sad days to grant wishes," the fairy said, "but if you'd have a reward, come to this place at midnight, and we will celebrate and give you what reward we can." Her voice seemed stronger and more confident, Amber noticed—either she was recovering quickly from her wounds, or this place, whatever it was, gave her courage.

"We don't need any reward," Amber said. "We just wanted to help you." She hesitated. "But we would like to see the others, you know, just to be sure you'll be safe here."

"Return at midnight, and you may see them."

"But I meant . . . Can't I see them now?"

"No. Go now," the fairy ordered. "Return at midnight, if you wish."

Uneasily, Amber backed out of the clearing in the hedge; reluctantly, Jason followed.

Charlie meowed at them from the porch; Amber turned to look at him, and when she turned back the opening in the hedge was gone.

She and Jason spent the better part of an hour exploring, walking up and down the hedge on either side, but they found no sign of an opening, nowhere that the hedge looked wide enough, front to back, to have contained the domelike clearing they remembered. They turned up nothing on the site of the gazebo but pillbugs. Turning, whirling, pacing, and jumping about did not cause the gap in the hedge to reappear.

Eventually they gave up and returned to the house, but Amber couldn't bring herself to pick up her abandoned book; instead she let Charlie in and sat in the windowseat on the stairway landing with the cat on her lap, petting him as she stared out across the back lawn at the garden and hedge.

"I love you, Charlie," she said, looking down at him, "but don't catch any more fairies, okay?"

The cat looked up at her with half-closed eyes and purred.

At supper neither Amber nor Jason mentioned anything of the day's events to their parents; they ate quietly, listening to chat about cars and jobs.

At bedtime that evening, as Amber let Charlie out for the night, Jason asked her, "So, you goin'?"

Amber nodded. "If I can stay awake," she said. "You?"

"Sure," Jason replied.

Amber lay in her bed with the lights out, thinking about the day.

She had always thought that their big old house looked like something out of a storybook, and that the semi-abandoned garden was especially spooky—but fairies? They seemed incredible.

She wasn't sure whether to be grateful that Charlie had caught the fairy, or worried. Charlie was a lovely cat, all sleek and black, and very friendly, but sometimes he could be so stubborn....

She didn't realize she had dozed off until Jason shook her awake. She sat up, startled.

"Come on!" he whispered. "It's only about five minutes till midnight!"

"Oh!" She jumped out of bed and shooed Jason out of the room so she could get dressed.

It was a good thing their parents hadn't stayed up late that night, Amber thought as she crept down the stairs.

Together she and Jason stumbled down the sloping yard to the garden, tripping over things in the dark. Everything seemed bigger, somehow—the hundred feet of lawn seemed like a thousand. At last, though, they arrived at the brick pillars that had held the garden gate, posts that normally barely reached Amber's waist—and they were over her head.

"Jason?" she said, looking up at the posts, their red brick black in the moonlight.

"We're shrinking," Jason said. "Down to fairy size, I guess—so we can celebrate with them."

Amber nodded.

"Come on," she said.

They made their way cautiously through the garden itself, and that walk was even worse, with the uneven bricks and the trailing vines and the tangled weeds and pricking thorns, all of them seemingly growing larger and larger as Amber and Jason proceeded, until by the time they reached the soft ground where the gazebo had stood it was a veritable jungle.

The hedge loomed over them, black in the darkness—black, solid, and impossibly tall.

"Now what?" Jason asked, staring at it.

"Now we take three steps and turn around," Amber said. "And if it doesn't work, we go back to bed, and I sure hope we grow back to normal size."

"I wish we'd taken a picture of the thing before we let it go," Jason muttered.

"A bit late to think of that," Amber retorted as she took her first step.

Then the second, the third; turn around...

And the hedge was alight with tiny glowing specks, like miniature candle flames, and the opening into the clearing had reappeared, a gigantic leafy archway outlined in flickering golden light.

" 'Tis the mortal children!" a voice called. "Make ready the feast! Those who saved Maurienne from the Beast are come!"

And then the fairies appeared on either side: long lines of them, almost as tall now as Amber and Jason, all of them inhumanly beautiful, with gleaming iridescent wings and radiant heart-shaped faces, long hair flowing down their backs. Their clothes were woven of spider silk and milkweed and a hundred other fine fibers, in shades of white and gray and gold. Two leaped forward and took Amber and Jason by the hand, and led them down between the lines as the fairies cheered wildly.

At the end they found a table, elaborately set with shining beetle-shell plates, acorn-cap bowls, thorn knives, and carved twig forks.

And on the other side of the table stood three fairies. In the center was the one they had rescued, her injured wing now bandaged with something green and white; to her right was a male fairy taller than any of the others, fully Amber's own shrunken height; while on Maurienne's left was a female fairy of Jason's current size.

The tall ones wore rings on their heads like crowns—a simple gold band on the male, while the female's had a diamond chip set in the front—and Amber realized these must be the king and queen; dredging up a memory from an old movie, she curtsied deeply, going down on one knee, wishing as she did so that she had worn a skirt instead of jeans. Jason, after a moment's befuddlement, picked up his cue and bowed.

"It's all like a story," Amber whispered as she rose. Jason nodded.

"Welcome to our home," the fairy king announced. "We do not ask your true names, as we seek no power over you; but what names shall we call you?"

Amber and Jason exchanged glances.

"Amber, Your Majesty," Amber said.

"Bill," Jason said.

Amber glared at him. "Bill?" she asked.

He shrugged and smiled sheepishly.

"Come then, Amber and Bill, and feast with us," the king proclaimed, "that we might honor you for what you did for our beloved subject, whom you rescued from that foul monster and brought safely home to us!"

Amber started to object that Charlie wasn't a monster, just a cat, *her* cat—but then she stopped herself. To these things, a cat *would* be a monster, and if she admitted Charlie was hers they'd hardly feel kindly toward her, would they?

The king waved a hand, and fairies began to load the table—which, Amber saw, was made of an old clapboard set up on chunks of two-by-four—with food. Nuts, berries, steaming chunks of meat—Amber wondered what sort of meat it was, but decided not to ask.

The acorn bowls were filled with golden wine—probably made from dandelions, Amber guessed.

She remembered stories of fairy feasts and of people being lost for years, or forever, if they ate so much as a bite—but this wasn't a story, this was real, strange as it seemed, and it would be rude not to eat.

Besides, the chance to bite into a strawberry the size of her own head was just too weird to miss. She and Jason, as directed, sat down on chairs made of empty wire spools and joined in.

As they ate, the fairies sang, and although Amber wasn't usually interested in folk music—she preferred Elastica—she enjoyed it immensely. Their voices were beautiful; about every third song was a funny one, and she laughed until she cried at those, though the minute each song ended she would never again remember any of the words or jokes.

Everything was delicious, everything was wonderful. Maurienne, if that was her name, stared across the table at Amber and Jason with a look of adoration that made Amber feel ten feet tall; the king and queen smiled proudly at them.

At last the feast was done and the dishes were cleared away; Amber felt full and sleepy and fine. The king and queen rose, and Amber remembered that she was supposed to stand as well; she got to her feet and stood, swaying slightly. Jason followed suit.

"And now," the king said, "the reward you were promised!"

He gestured, and Amber felt something touching her shoulders; she turned, startled, and found that two fairies had come up behind her and draped a cloak across her shoulders.

Two others had done the same for Jason.

"Cool," he said.

Amber, tired as she was, tried to focus on the cloak that covered her shoulders.

It was fur, fine black fur; she stroked it.

It was sleek and soft and smooth.

It felt somehow familiar.

"What kind is it?" Jason asked as Amber looked up, horrified, at the king's smiling face.

He had canines almost like fangs, she noticed for the first time, and the queen's smile was equally sinister; the two were leering, mocking.

"Why, you said that the reward you asked was to see us all safe," the king replied. "This cloak is the sign of our safety, now and forever, from the Beast that savaged Maurienne. What else would be fitting for your cloaks but the Beast's own hide?"

"What?" Jason said. His face went pale, but Amber didn't notice.

"Charlie!" she shrieked.

And then the fairies and the candles and the table, the king and queen and everything else, vanished, and Amber and Jason were kneeling together in the moonlight in the weeds behind the garden, each of them clutching a scrap of their cat's skin.

NINA KIRIKI HOFFMAN

WONDER NEVER LAND

"Are we there yet?" my little brother, Bradley, asked for the two hundredth time, tugging on Mom's braid where it hung down over the seat back. I didn't know how he could be so energetic so early in the morning. Wonder Never Land was two hours from our town, and we'd gotten up at six to get there before it opened and before the crowds.

I figured Bradley was one reason we'd never gone to

Wonder Never Land before. It was hard being in a car with him for fifteen minutes, let alone two hours.

"Ten more minutes," said Dad, from the driver's seat, "and stop pulling your mother's hair—how many times do I have to tell you?"

"What I wouldn't give for ten minutes of peace," Mom said, trying to pull her braid out of Bradley's grip. Tugging anything out of Bradley's grip was difficult. Once Bradley got hold of something it could take a natural disaster to make him let go.

Something in Mom's tone of voice when she talked about peace made me shiver. It was more than just being at the end of her rope. It was, *I've run out of rope, and now I'm falling.*

But I couldn't talk to Bradley about that. I used to try. I used to say, "Can't you just let up, even for one day?"

"What?" he would say. "What, what? Like I'm doing something wrong? And who are you to tell me what to do, Princess Sarah Shiver-in-Her-Boots?"

"Are we there yet?" Bradley asked again. Since he couldn't hang on to Mom's hair, he pinched me instead.

If I slapped him he would just pinch harder, so I hunched away from him and up against the window. He was ten and I was twelve, but he was almost as big as I was.

"Stop it," I said. But not like I meant it. Bradley never listened anyway.

Four "Are we there yet?"s later, Dad said, "We're here. We're here!"

And there was the gate, just the way I'd seen it in the commercials. Two giant pirates brandishing

45

cutlasses held up one end of the big log over the turn-in to Wonder Never Land, and a big gorilla and a huge dinosaur held up the other end. Beyond them and the parking lot we could see the top loops of the roller coasters, the gleaming tracks of the elevated monorail that circled the park, and the spires of the Haunted Castle. Everything was frozen and quiet.

Right in the middle of Wonder Never Land stood a tall green-and-brown mountain with a snowy white top. Shining tracks eeled in and out of the mountain's sides like big silver earthworms.

Bradley chanted, "Abracadabra Fantasti-Ride!" We'd seen the ride in commercials for Wonder Never Land. It had just opened a month earlier. Everyone was talking about it, but nobody we knew had gone on it yet.

Dad turned the car in through the gate. I looked up at the huge pirates as we drove past them. If I had a sword that big I would smack Bradley a good one with the flat of the blade.

Bradley bared his teeth at me and clacked them together. I knew he was being Godzilla. Thoughts of him biting chunks of flesh out of my arm chased away thoughts of my imaginary sword.

It made me mad. How come Bradley's imagination could always eclipse mine?

Even though we were so early, we had to park way far away from the entrance and take a shuttle bus. There were already lots of other cars frying in the summer sun.

In the front seat of the shuttle bus sat Slithery the Snake, one of the mascots of Wonder Never. His upper body rose from a nest of coils on the seat, and his head was as high as a grown-up's. His tail lapped over the edge of the seat and draped down, kinking at the end where it touched the floor. He had a white belly, and black and orange diamonds down his back. His golden eyes were as big as my hand. They had thin black up-and-down pupil slits in the centers.

I thought at first maybe he was just a big old stuffed animal coiled on the seat, but as I walked past him his head turned, and a black ribbon tongue flicked out of his mouth. Its forked tip touched my cheek. I shivered.

Bradley laughed. "Snake slobber, snake slobber!" Bradley yelled, making everybody on the bus turn to look at us. Mom put her hands on my shoulders and steered me toward an empty seat.

My cheek burned a little where the black tongue had touched me. As Mom and I sat down, I brushed the hot spot on my face with a finger.

"Don't," said Mom. "There's a red star on your cheek now. Maybe it's good luck."

Dad shoved Bradley into a seat behind us. I lowered my hand, but I could feel a blush heating my cheeks. I didn't really want to walk around with a star on my face. I didn't like it when people looked at me. It always made me feel like I had a giant zit, or maybe some mustard smeared across my chin.

When we got out of the bus, though, one of the squeaky clean orange-suited Wonder People came up to us and led us right past all the lines of people waiting to pay for tickets. "You have a blessing star," she said to me, and smiled, showing a mouthful of teeth so white it was almost like staring at a lightbulb. "That means free admission for you, and front of the line for the rest of your family."

"Give me that star!" Bradley yelled, scratching my cheek.

Mom pulled his hand away. I clapped my hand to my cheek, wondering if the star were still there. The Wonder Person still smiled with her mouthful of light, blinking her big bright eyes.

"Don't worry," she said in her radio-commercial voice, "blessings don't come off." She smiled even wider. She looked at Bradley. Her smile didn't waver. Then she turned and led us to a ticket booth that had been roped off. It had no line in front of it. Dad went right up to the ticket window and bought tickets for himself and Mom and Bradley. They all got their hands stamped, but I didn't have to.

The Wonder Person led us to the big barred gates into Wonder Never Land, and she pulled them inward, opening a space just wide enough for us to get in. It was an hour before the actual opening time of the park, but my star let us in ahead of all the others.

The Wonder Person smiled again.

"Welcome to Wonder Never Land, Special Person," she said to me, "and welcome, Special Person's family."

Bradley didn't say anything until she'd pulled the gates closed behind herself and was facing all the other ticket holders, who waited behind furry orange ropes for the *Come in* signal.

Special Person, I thought. Nobody had ever called me that. I got good grades. I didn't make a lot of noise. My hair was dirt brown and my face looked like sidekick material. When I was at home Bradley was always the center of attention, and when I was at school there were other people who shone and other people who made a lot of noise. No one ever noticed me.

I kind of liked it like that. I was used to it. I wasn't sure about this new world order.

"Special Person," Bradley said. "Yeah, right." He flicked his middle finger against the hot star spot on my cheek, stinging me, and sauntered on ahead.

Mom stroked my hair. "Don't let it bother you, Sarah," she said. She said that a lot. I wasn't sure how to obey her. I peeked up past my bangs at her. She smiled wide, and said, "Really. I mean it this time."

"Abra-cadabra-Fantasti-Ride," Bradley chanted as we headed past giants and dinosaurs and fairies and elves and knights. We had the park to ourselves, except for grinning Wonder People near the entrance to every ride. Everything looked clean and fresh. There were food booths beside the walkways, with people inside them getting ready for the rush. I could smell hot dogs cooking and taste cotton candy on the air, and those big elephant-ear pastries, and pretzels. A woman in a glass-sided cart that sold popcorn and pink lemonade grinned at me. She was dressed like the women in old western movies.

We approached a carousel with all kinds of strange, brightly painted animals on it: sea monsters, winged horses, a giant earthworm, a big black-and-yellow spotted salamander. I really wanted to go on that one, even though Bradley said carousels were for babies. I touched Mom's hand and pointed. She smiled. "Let's try this one," she said to Dad and Bradley.

"Bor-ing! For babies!" Bradley yelled. "Abra-cadabra!"

"We're doing the Abracadabra Fantasti-Ride last," Dad said.

"I want to do it *now*," said Bradley.

"Too bad," said Mom.

Usually when we got to this point in discussions, Bradley would yell and scream awhile and then everyone would give in, but not this time.

This time Mom ignored Bradley's yells and walked to the carousel gate. I went with her, feeling warmth in my stomach because for once I got first choice. I looked at all the animals: a pouncing tiger, a white horse with garlands of flowers twisted into its flying mane and tail, a silver swan with an arched neck. There was no one else around; I could ride on any animal I liked—unless I picked the one Bradley wanted. I thought I should pick an animal I didn't like first, since that would be the one he wanted, and then I could switch to my own favorite.

"Welcome, Special People!" said the Wonder Person at the gate. I blushed. I had forgotten about my star. The Wonder Person was a young man with short blond hair and another shiny wide smile. He showed us a lot of teeth and took the orange velvet rope out of the way to let us onto the carousel.

"You can ride the dumb old merry-go-round," Bradley said suddenly. "I'm not going to waste my time! I'm going on the Abracadabra Fantasti-Ride right now, before there's a line!" He ran away.

Dad said, "Eileen, you and Sarah go ahead. Ride the carousel. I'll catch him." He ran off after Bradley.

Just try to take a first choice away from Bradley, I

thought. *He'll never let that happen.* I tried to smile at the Wonder Person as Mom and I walked past him, but Bradley's running away had kind of taken the fun out of it, even though he probably would have been miserable on the carousel.

"Come on, Sarah. Which animal do you like?" Mom asked.

I saw a Slithery the Snake, all orange and black diamonds along his three-humped back, with a saddle on the first hump behind his head. Slithery had gotten me into this. Might as well ride him. I wondered if he went up and down on his post, or what? I looked into one golden eye and then put my foot into the stirrup of his saddle and climbed on his back, grabbing the pole right in front of the saddle.

"Are you sure that's the one you want?" asked Mom. "There's no one else. You could ride any animal at all." As if she knew I always had last choice at everything.

I looked at the tiger, and the lion with the long mane and crown of daisies, and the black stallion with the silver bells twined into his mane, and the sphinx with her front paws up, claws extended. I liked all the other animals. All of them were bright and unchipped, and they all had glass eyes that shone like life in the morning light.

I patted Slithery's scaled back. "I want this one," I said.

Mom shrugged and got onto the prancing rabbit next to Slithery. "You're the boss," she said.

"Ready?" asked the Wonder Person. We both nodded, and he turned a crank. Music that sounded like it came from clown instruments and glass bells started, and the carousel began to turn. Slithery's humps moved up and down, rippling, his tail flicking behind me. He felt alive under me. I gripped the pole and laughed. Mom's rabbit hopped. I looked toward the mosaic of crystal mirrors and golden genie faces at the center of the carousel, where the music came from, and watched me and Mom bobbing up and down. Mom was smiling. My short dark hair streamed behind my head. I couldn't stop laughing. The carousel spun faster and faster, making me dizzy, till I couldn't look past the bobbing animals around me at the outside world because it was spinning by too quickly.

I wished we could stay on the carousel forever, in this bubble of motion and music, just us. No outside world. No loud whining Bradley.

Finally the carousel slowed and stopped. "Where's my stomach?" Mom said. "I didn't know a merry-go-round could be so exciting!" She patted her rabbit.

I kissed Slithery's nose. I could swear his big golden eye winked at me, even though I knew snakes didn't have eyelids.

Dad and Bradley were standing outside the gate. Dad had his hand around Bradley's wrist. Bradley wore a big scowl.

"What would you like to do next, Sarah?" Mom asked.

Me picking twice in a row? I didn't think so. "It's Bradley's turn to pick," I said.

"Bradley lost his turn when he ran away," said Dad.

Bradley would take his turn anyway, I thought. "The Haunted Castle," I said. Kids at school always talked about the Haunted Castle. They used to say it was the best ride in the whole park—at least until the Abracadabra Fantasti-Ride opened.

"The Haunted Castle? *Ach-ptoooiiee!*" Bradley said.

"Would you like to change your mind?" Dad asked Bradley. "We're going no matter how you feel, but it would be nice if you could be enthusiastic about something that wasn't your idea."

Bradley stared up at Dad with slitted eyes, and muttered, "Abracadabra," under his breath.

The magic word. I wondered what he was pretending to turn Dad into.

"Last chance," Dad said. Something in the way he said it sounded strange to me, as if these were words of lead he was speaking instead of words of air. If I had been Bradley, I would have listened. I would have heard the weight. I would have done the best I could to change my mind and at least act as if the Haunted Castle were the place on Earth I most wanted to go.

But Bradley was never very good at listening to things. He made his lips disappear into a frown and then stared at the ground. Dad had to drag him to the Haunted Castle.

It was almost nine o'clock. In a minute the gates would open and floods of people would come in. Lines would form, and the longest line of all would be at the Abracadabra Fantasti-Ride. It was in all the commercials. It was new. Even people who had come to Wonder Never Land a hundred times had never been on it. And this was the middle of summer, when people were on vacation and came from all over the country to go to Wonder Never Land.

We could be at the head of that line if I just said the word. Bradley would be happy for a few minutes. I wouldn't have to worry about what he might do to me later for not doing what he wanted. I could be the me I always was, and cave in.

I touched the star on my cheek where Slithery had licked me, and I remembered the Wonder Person at the gate telling me I was special. I didn't really want to go on the Abracadabra Fantasti-Ride. I don't like roller coasters. They scare me more than most other things.

"Sarah?" said Mom.

"You and I could go to the Haunted Castle, and Dad and Bradley could go on the Fantasti-Ride," I said.

"Castle first, Fantasti-Ride second," Dad said.

I loved the Haunted Castle. I can't explain this, but there are some things that scare me and I love them, and some things that scare me and I hate them. I loved it when we went down in a spidery black elevator and all of a sudden all the people on the elevator with us turned into skeletons. Then when we climbed into the giant black baby carriages at the bottom and they carried us past a cemetery full of ghosts and through a grove of talking trees, right through the middle of a gunfight on an old western street, and along beside a river where a girl jumped off a bridge and turned into a ghost as she hit the water—and all the ghosts were in costumes of long ago, and the baby carriages looked like antiques left by giants, and everything was dark except things that glowed in the dark, and a whole raft of bats flew over our heads so low I thought one was going to hit me....I loved all that even while I was shivering.

We rode past a saloon where men were playing poker, and just as we got there two of them jumped up and shot each other, then collapsed. The one nearest the track leaned over and said, "You're next," right in my face, while blood was pouring out of the hole in his shirt, and I screamed and screamed.

I loved it.

We went right through the center of an old stone room with a round table in it, and all these suits of armor jumped to their feet and saluted us with swords. Then the armor fell all to pieces and only skeletons were standing there, holding swords out and laughing like fiends and demons. I screamed some more.

Finally the baby carriages burped out through rusty iron gates that looked like they led into a mausoleum but instead carried us blinking out into the sunshine, where Wonder People were waiting to help us up out of our vehicles.

"That was great," I said to Mom, to Dad. They smiled. "That was great," I told the Wonder People, who smiled, too. "Thanks!"

Bradley didn't say anything. He was still scowling. I figured maybe he had enjoyed it a little, or he would have been making more noise.

Off in the distance I could see that the loops of roller coasters had cars on them now. People were screaming all over Wonder Never Land in fear and delight. There was a hum to the place that meant it was occupied by others now, not just Wonder People and us. It was as if the park were breathing in and out instead of frozen.

"Where now, Sarah?" asked Dad.

"It's Bradley's turn to pick." Dad was making me

nervous, asking me what I wanted. At home he almost never did. Bradley got to control the remote. Bradley got to pick the games. Bradley got to practice on the piano first, and Bradley got to pick the book Mom would read out loud to us. I used to try to fight Bradley about all these things, but it got so it was more trouble to fight than give in, and if I didn't like what Bradley picked, I could always go up to my room and read or paint my D&D figures and make them act out stories and campaigns.

"Sarah, what do you want to do next?" Mom asked, as though I were a Special Person still.

"Abracadabra Fantasti-Ride," I said, even though it was the last ride in the park I wanted to go on.

So we walked toward the mountain in the middle of Wonder Never Land. The mountain grew as we walked toward it. It had looked brown and green and white from a distance, but as we got closer I could see there was a whole jungle on the lower slopes, full of trees cloaked with bright-flowered vines. Big white long-armed monkeys with black faces swung through the trees. Orchids and other flowers that looked like mutations grew in the crotches of the trees, and the leaves on the trees were all fringed and lace edged, like paper snowflakes. Waterfalls tumbled down the side of the mountain. In the shadows of the jungle, large dark creatures moved and grunted and barked. None of them sounded like dogs, or any other animal I knew. I saw light glint on long icicle teeth.

The roller coaster tracks burst from the mountainside, slid through pieces of jungle, and plunged into the mountain again. Trains zipped past on the tracks, with people all openmouthed and screaming.

I gripped Mom's hand tighter. I really did not want to go on this ride. But I knew Bradley wanted to do it, and I knew everybody would ask us about it when we went back to school on Monday. How bad could it be? Nobody had ever died on a ride at Wonder Never Land, at least not that I had heard.

I knew it was safe, but I was glad to see that the line to get on was already really long. We went and stood at the end.

I watched people getting off. Their cheeks were red, and their eyes glowed. The entire inside of the mountain was full of screaming, but people were going on the ride, and the same people were getting off at the other end. I timed it. It took twelve minutes.

The line wound around outside the bottom of the mountain. Mom put sunblock on me and would have put some on Bradley, but he squirmed away when she tried. She even put some on the part in my hair.

Then the line went inside the mountain. We were in a tunnel that looked like a mine. Jewels gleamed from the ceiling, and threads of gold and silver veined the walls. Bradley tried to pull a gold vein out, but Dad slapped his hand. A Wonder Person was watching us. He smiled at me when he saw my star.

A window beside the path showed a drop where the roller coaster zoomed by every once in a while as I watched. People held their arms up in the air and screamed. Most of them were smiling.

After about an hour, during which Bradley told me

in a whisper about sixty times that we could have ridden this twice if I hadn't been so stupid about the dumb carousel (he didn't mention the Haunted Castle, though, so I knew he had liked it), we finally reached the head of the line.

Dad talked to the Wonder Person who was lifting the orange velvet rope to let people onto the roller coaster cars. "Special ticket," Dad said, reaching a hand out.

The Wonder Person took something from Dad and peeked at it, then put it in her pocket and nodded. She signaled to another Wonder Person, who smiled and came over to us.

"We've got a special treat for you," said this guy to me and Bradley.

"Go on," said Dad, smiling.

"Aren't you coming?" I looked up at Mom, then at Dad.

"No, this ride is just for you."

"But I don't—"

Mom stroked my hair. "Go on, Sarah. It will be all right."

I let go of her hand. She had told me that before. Usually it wasn't true. But I didn't want to spoil things the way Bradley did by holding back or being a whiner. We had gotten this far. Might as well go all the way. I could always close my eyes and just hang on tight and wait. It would be over in twelve minutes. I could stand that.

"C'mon," said the Wonder Person, treating us to another blinding grin.

"Is this some kind of gyp?" Bradley asked as we

walked down a dark tunnel and away from the main tracks. "Are we getting some kind of cheap shortcut ride? We paid the full price! At least, I did. My stupid sister, Sarah, got that star, but it's not my fault!"

"This ride is *better* than the regular ride," said the Wonder Person.

We came to a cave with green sparkles all over the walls. Sitting there was a single roller coaster car, just big enough for two people. The track in front of it led straight up into darkness.

"No," I moaned. Up meant down, sooner or later. Dark meant you wouldn't be able to tell ahead of time. It was worse than most of my nightmares, and I had a lot of those.

The Wonder Person patted my shoulder and pushed the safety bar back. Bradley jumped into the car and shoved over to the far side.

I looked at the Wonder Person. He smiled and lifted his eyebrows. I looked at the restraint bar. It was bright chrome and looked really sturdy. Even if the car fell apart, I could hang on to it.

I climbed onto the seat next to Bradley, and the Wonder Person pushed the safety bar down until it was tight against our stomachs. I gripped it so hard my hands hurt.

The Wonder Person went over to a big orange lever. He talked on a walkie-talkie to someone, watched his watch, and, nodding his head, pulled the lever.

The car Bradley and I were in shot up into darkness, leaving my stomach behind. "Yesssss," Bradley hissed beside me.

There was a clanking sound under us. We just kept

rising and rising through darkness. The air was cool and smelled like a storm. Far away, I could hear muffled screaming from other people.

"This is great. This is so great," Bradley said in the darkness. "Oh, this is great! Just wait'll we go down, Sarah. You'll be tossing cookies right and left!"

"No, just right—on you," I said. My voice came out all tight and small.

"Good one," said Bradley, and punched me on the arm.

Then the car crested and stopped.

I couldn't hear anything. We were just sitting there in the cool darkness. I couldn't hear the regular roller coasters or screams or even any machinery.

I began to think about spiders. Big ones.

There could be webs right above our heads. Really big spiders might even eat kids. First sting you silly so you couldn't move, then spit this stuff into you that turned your guts to liquid, then suck you dry, leaving a crackly skin outline of you. But you wouldn't actually die until after the gut-sucking part.

"Shiver-in-Her-Boots does it again," Bradley said, and laughed really loud, like a donkey. I wanted to smack him, but I couldn't get my fingers to let go of the chrome safety bar.

A little green light bobbed toward us out of the darkness. I began to relax away from the total tension and paralysis, because as the light approached I could see that there weren't any spiders above me.

A boy was carrying the light. He was dressed, for a wonder, in green.

"Listen," he said as he got close.

I listened. I wasn't ready to do anything else.

"This is your chance," he said.

"Chance for what, dweeb?" said Bradley.

"This is your chance to get out of it all and come to a place where there aren't any grown-ups, where no one tells you what to do. You can eat all the sweets you want. You can stay up as long as you want. You can watch as much TV as you want. We live in the mountain. There's a whole complex in here just for kids. It goes way down in the ground. We can come out at night and ride the rides as many times as we like. I've been here two years already. It's great."

"All I want to do is ride *this* ride," Bradley said.

"You can ride it over and over again," said the boy. "Later. It's better after dark, believe me."

"I want to ride it *now*."

"Now is your only chance to get off and stay," the boy said. "You can only ride the Limited once. If you go on with the ride and get off at the end like everybody else, nobody's heard of us, there's nothing in here like I just told you, it's all a big fantasy you made up. This is it, kid. Your only chance. Yes or no?"

"Over and over?" Bradley asked. "This ride?"

"You got it," said the boy. "Sister, you want to stay with us? Big fun! Oh no. You got the star." He frowned at me, shining the light toward my face. "Never mind."

"The star means she can't stay?" Bradley said.

"Some grown-up gave her the star. She's too goody-goody to stick around."

"I could stay, but she can't?"

"She could if she wanted to, but she won't want to."

I thought about that. I resented this boy deciding

that I wouldn't want to live a life where everything was fun all the time. Imagine being able to ride every animal on the carousel, or going through the Haunted Castle enough times to learn all the ghosts by name. Not to mention all the other rides we hadn't even tried yet.

But I didn't want to leave Mom and Dad. I didn't want to quit school. I even knew I would get homesick for my bedroom if I got off this ride and off the world as I knew it. No way did I want to stay here in the dark.

"Shiver-Sis, that true?" Bradley asked.

"I don't want to stay here."

"Har!" said Bradley. He shoved at the safety bar. "Let me off. I'm ready for a world without a sister in it!"

"You sure?" said the kid. "Absolutely, positively sure?"

"Yep," said Bradley.

The boy came forward and twisted something behind us. The chrome bar swung away from our laps, and Bradley climbed out over me.

I felt strange in my stomach, as though I'd swallowed something cold and dead. "Don't," I whispered. I wouldn't miss Bradley . . . would I?

"Give it up," Bradley said. "Hey, kid, lead me to the ice cream! How many flavors you got?"

"At least fifty. Anything we ask for," said the boy. He twisted something in the car and the chrome bar dropped in my lap again. The boy smiled at me once, waved with the hand away from Bradley. "Ready?" he asked me.

I clutched the bar. I looked at my brother. What would Mom and Dad say? This would never work. They would talk to the police. They would tear the park apart. They would blame me for losing my brother.

"It'll be okay," the boy said softly.

I shook my head.

"It will. Ready?"

I waited a minute. Bradley was already heading down the hall that the boy had come from. I nodded.

The boy talked into something on his wrist, waited a few seconds, then pulled a lever like the one the Wonder Person had pulled to start us on this ride. The car jerked and clanged ahead on the tracks, leading to the inevitable downslide straight into nothingness.

I screamed and closed my eyes and screamed some more as the car jerked sideways, up, down; slid straight and curved. I could tell from the air on my face that the car was going outside the mountain and back in; it changed from warm to cool to warm. I could see light through my closed eyelids, and then darkness. I could hear the other people screaming over my own scream, and sometimes I could smell the park again, popcorn and machine oil and hot dogs, people and plants. Sometimes I heard the mechanical animals in the jungle hoot and call and bark.

The car went down and down and down, air whooshing past my face, my chest; my stomach tried to crowd up my throat. I opened my mouth and screamed some more, wondering if I could actually cough up my guts the way I felt like I wanted to. Then there was this huge clanking noise, and the car rammed into something, but almost immediately it slowed. I heard people near me saying, "What a rush! Let's do it again! Can you believe it?"

I opened my eyes and found that my car had attached to a train that had a bunch of other cars in it already, and we pulled into the disembarkation platform, and Wonder People ran up to us, released the chrome bars, and helped staggering people to their feet.

I felt pale and cold, as if no force on Earth would stop me from throwing up. A Wonder Person handed me a cup full of liquid. "Sip this," she murmured to me. I tasted it and my stomach settled right away, even though the liquid tasted like raspberry cough syrup. She patted my shoulder. "Not your favorite ride, huh?"

"I hated it," I said.

"Not my favorite, either," she said. She took my arm and helped me away from the train and down some steps.

Mom and Dad were waiting there. They looked solemn.

Now it starts, I thought. I sipped some more raspberry. The Wonder Person stroked my back and headed off.

"You didn't like that ride at all, did you?" asked Mom.

"No," I said.

"You don't ever have to go on it again," Dad said.

"Mom— Dad— Bradley, he—"

"Hush, Sarah."

"But in the mountain, this boy—"

"It's all right."

"But—"

"It's all right, Sarah. Do you want to go on any other rides?" Mom asked.

I clutched my stomach. I wasn't even sure I wanted to get in the car again. Besides, they couldn't just ignore the fact that Bradley was gone.

"Can we just sit down for a minute?" I asked.

"Sure," said Dad. He led the way to a table shaped like a toadstool, under an umbrella like a big banana leaf. We sat on shorter red toadstools with white spots.

"Bradley—" I said.

"There is no Bradley," said Dad.

When we got home, Bradley's room was full of exercise equipment. There weren't any of his toys anywhere that I could ever find, or his clothes. Even the pictures on the wall of the stairwell had no Bradleys in them. The ones I remembered of us as a family, where Bradley was always making horrible faces and sticking rabbit ears behind my head—those were all gone. There were just pictures of me, and Mom, and Dad.

The few times I tried to talk about it, Dad said, "You have no brother."

Sometimes after I turn out the light I lie in bed and think about this. It occurs to me that there can't be a huge underground complex beneath the Abracadabra Fantasti-Ride—at least, not one that's been there for two years. The ride just opened. What if everything the kid with the light said was a lie? What if Bradley went down that dark tunnel and fell forever?

I didn't hear him scream. That's the thought I hug

to myself. That's the thought that finally lets me sleep.

It occurs to me that maybe there never was a Bradley.

I can still see that bruise on my arm where Bradley pinched me, though. I can see it in the Polaroid one of the Wonder People took of me as I left the park—it shows up just as clear as that blessing star on my cheek.

Sometimes I laugh too loud, or complain about something, or ask Mom for something three times in a row even though she says no. Then I see her look at Dad, and he looks at her. Their eyebrows go up and then down.

That's when it occurs to me maybe I better shut up and be good. If Dad could get a special ticket once, why not twice?

MARK A. GARLAND

INTO THE GAP

Emil turned the corner onto Pine Road and started ped-aling hard. Already the autumn days were getting much shorter, the sun was rising later, and the winds were blowing colder. This morning the sky was full of thick black clouds. The wind gusted, swirling leaves into his path, and he could smell the coming rain in the air. This far out in the country there weren't any streetlights, not until

Pine Road ran into Route 4, near the middle school.

Pine Road was a spooky place to begin with. He always felt a little uneasy riding this stretch, even though he'd done it a thousand times. But today was the worst yet. He couldn't remember ever riding to school in such gloomy darkness.

Emil usually had a little help seeing where he was going, from the headlights of passing cars, but none had passed him so far today. Which was strange all by itself.

He wanted a headlight for his bike—and a new bike to put it on, since his was getting pretty bad. It only had two of the original ten speeds, and one of the rims was bent. The faster you went, the more the bike shook.

He had a birthday coming up, but he was pretty sure a new bike was out of the question, at least right now. And rough as the bike was, it was better than nothing.

When he got all the way to the corner of Route 4 he didn't find any traffic there, either, and he decided he was probably just running a bit early. But the Mobil station on the corner looked deserted, and even the sign that read OPEN 24 HOURS was out.

Emil pulled his bike over, fighting with the shift lever to get it in low gear, then he sat for a while, staring at a road that should have had cars coming and going on it. *Not one,* he thought. Which, of course, was just about impossible.

He finally decided to just keep going to the school. If anything strange were happening, they'd know about it there. Ms. Gilman, the principal, would certainly know. She never missed a thing. Emil was convinced she was out to get him. She seemed to know everything about everyone. She was always in the right place at the right time, always knew who had done what. It was a little weird, really.

Emil had been trying hard to stay out of trouble, and out of Ms. Gilman's way, especially lately. His mother had enough problems right now, enough to make her cry, sometimes. His parents had both lost their jobs when the bottling plant closed down. They didn't have many options. In fact, they could only think of one. Emil's father had taken a job down south.

They would all be together again eventually, when his father got enough money saved, but it seemed to be taking an awfully long time. Emil was pretty sure his mother missed his father almost as much as he did, and having her son suspended from school would only make things worse.

Sometimes, though, it seemed like getting into trouble was just what happened when he tried to fit in. Nobody had ever gotten hurt, even when he'd pulled a couple of real no-brainers, even the time Annie Frith told him she'd go to the movies with him if he'd sneak into the main office and set off the school's fire alarm. It hadn't been easy; the lever was right in plain sight on the wall, just inside the door. Emil was fast, though. He'd managed to reach in at just the right moment, when the secretary wasn't looking. . . .

Anyway, Ms. Gilman said she would find out who had done it, and Emil was still worried she would. On top of all that, Annie Frith had somehow managed to be busy every night and every weekend ever since.

As Emil pulled into the school circle and headed for the bike racks he noticed there weren't any other bikes there, and no cars in the teacher's parking lot, and no school buses dropping anybody off. The lights inside were on, but he couldn't see anyone moving around. *It's Saturday,* Emil thought, *or an emergency! One I don't know about!*

But his mother listened to the radio every morning before school, and there hadn't been any news. Not that news made a difference to her day. She only went somewhere when she had a job interview. Or when a check came from Emil's father, and they went to do the shopping. And the neighbors had gone to work as usual, so all this just didn't make any sense.

Emil parked the bike—he didn't bother locking it up, no one would bother to steal it—then he walked up to the school's front doors and looked inside. No one there. He tried the doors and found them locked.

Should be daylight by now, he worried, looking into the bleak night behind him. Then he heard a sound up the road, getting louder. A car came into view and turned into the circle, then slowly pulled up to the curb right in front of the school.

The engine shut off and the driver's door opened. Emil waited, tensing up, ready to run if he had to. He was just about to make a break for it when he realized it was Ms. Gilman. As she came toward him he saw her eyes, and he decided she looked different somehow. Not her usual diabolically cheerful self. The cheerful part was missing.

"Emil, how did you get here?" she asked, frowning, which in fact was something she had a talent for.

"I rode my bike."

Ms. Gilman's frown deepened. "That's not what I

meant. Tell me, have you seen anyone else, anyone at all?"

"No."

"Good," she said slowly, then her look changed. "I thought we expelled you after that fire alarm incident."

"Not me," Emil said, just looking at her. *Not yet, anyway,* he thought. She glanced over her shoulder, then she looked down at Emil again. She had started smiling just a little bit, which was frightening. Possibly even more frightening than the darkness and the wind and the empty streets.

"Maybe...maybe there's an emergency," Emil offered. "Was there any news on the car radio?"

Ms. Gilman shook her head. "No, I'm afraid not."

"I think I'd better call my mom," Emil said.

"Sure," Ms. Gilman said, rattling a handful of keys, grinning for certain now. "Let's go inside."

Emil looked in through the glass doors and down the brightly lit hallway that led past the main office while Ms. Gilman put a key in the lock. She tugged the big glass doors open, and they pushed inside. Then she locked the doors behind her. "I'm afraid you'll have to remain here for now," she said as she turned toward him. "And the phones won't work, not for you. I don't think you'll be talking to anyone from your world again for quite a while."

Emil wanted to think Ms. Gilman was kidding around, but he had never known her to kid before. Not once. "What do you mean?" he asked.

"It's unfortunate, but this sort of thing happens now and then," Ms. Gilman said. "For now just consider yourself a...a missing person."

"Who's missing?" Emil asked, afraid of the answer.

Ms. Gilman leaned toward him. "You are."

"I am not!"

"You are."

Emil felt his insides sag toward his Reeboks. "Where did I...go?"

"Tell me, Emil, have you ever imagined, even once, even for just a moment, that the whole world is really a gigantic experiment of some kind? That it's all been set up by a committee of advanced beings, just like an amusement park, or a zoo habitat perhaps, and most of the people you see are fake? Or that they are some of 'them'? Except you, of course, and a few others—probably your mom, maybe your father. You are the object of the whole thing, the point of the experiment. The victim. Most everyone else is just watching to see what *you* will do."

Emil stood there utterly stunned. He *had* felt that way, and more than once. But he'd never imagined...

Emil nodded quietly.

"Then you understand," Ms. Gilman said.

Emil just stared at her.

"You're speechless, aren't you?" Ms. Gilman said, patting Emil on the head. "That's sweet. That's what we like about you, and the others like you, of course. Fascinating bunch."

"We are?"

"Yes. I've been watching you for a few years now, and writing my reports has been something of a joy. Sometimes they let me use my codes to modify the experiment. You know, make this happen, prevent that from happening, just to see what effect it will have on you. Have you noticed how sometimes it seems like you can study like crazy and still only get a *B*, while the next kid keeps getting *A*s all the time, and you never see him studying at all? Well, I'm doing that."

Emil let his mouth hang open. "You are?"

"Of course. Those kids who seem like they're perfect, like they aren't even human—they aren't! We have other means at our disposal as well, of course. Basically, I can fix, ruin, or just change most anything."

Emil was beginning to grasp the implications of what Ms. Gilman was saying, but the more he thought about them, the harder they were to imagine.

"Did you make the bottling plant close?"

"Oh, that. No, but it has made things more interesting, hasn't it? I love surprises."

I used to, Emil thought. He asked the most important question next: "What are you going to do with me? What have you done with the others like me?"

Ms. Gilman reached out and grabbed Emil's arm with an iron grip, then she started walking up the hallway, leaving Emil no choice but to tag along. "It's a little bit complicated," she said.

"Tell me anyway," Emil said, pulling back and dragging his feet in protest.

Ms. Gilman stopped and glared at him. For an instant he thought she was going to break his arm. Then she sighed. "I suppose I may as well," she agreed, so Emil started walking again.

"Now and then the equipment breaks, and we have to shut everything down temporarily, in order to make repairs," she explained. "When that happens, we put most everyone 'real' into suspension with a Beta-Four

73

Multidimensional Subquantum Crossaxial Polynominal Nucleonic Dampening Field, deluxe model four. It's a hunk of junk, though, if you ask me. Of course you already know that."

"I do?"

"It's obvious, isn't it? The field has gaps, weak spots, like that one section of Pine Road you were no doubt pedaling down this morning."

Emil felt awful. "Oh," he said. There was too much to think about, too much all at once.

They arrived at the principal's office. Ms. Gilman stepped inside, pulling Emil with her; then she closed the door and locked it. The other office doors were all closed tight. There was nowhere to go. She let go of Emil's arm and picked up the phone on the secretary's desk. She fished in her purse for a moment and retrieved a small black disk the size of a quarter, which she stuck on the phone's receiver. She punched in a number at least twenty digits long.

"Can't you just put me back when you get the machines working again?" Emil asked while they stood there waiting.

Ms. Gilman looked down at him, but her eyes seemed to focus on something far away. "Emil," she said, "if I let you do that, even knowing what little you know, you'd ruin the experiment. If you knew any more, why, you'd probably take over the world!" She laughed out loud at this, focusing again, then she shook her head. "Of course, you'd need to know the code system to do that, and that's just—"

She cut herself off. "Yes, I've got a code fourteen," she said into the phone to someone, somewhere. "Emil.

He's the middle-school kid." She waited a moment, then nodded, and punched four more digits into the phone before hanging up.

"They're sending a replacement," she said. "A car will bring him here in a few minutes. We always keep a few on hand. Halfheads, we call them. Their minds are specially prepared with only a little basic knowledge. We copy all your thoughts into his head, then he goes home on your bike while you go back to the center in the car for reprocessing. Of course you won't be aware by then. And soon enough your mind will be wiped clean of everything that's happened today."

Emil gulped hard. " 'Wiped clean'?"

Ms. Gilman nodded. "After we copy your memories into the double, he will be you. Eventually we'll put you back, provided nothing goes wrong."

" 'Goes wrong'?" Emil asked, feeling his throat getting tighter.

"We lose a few, now and then, but many do survive the process and never remember any of it. We do it all the time. We have centers set up all over the world. Actually, the process isn't perfect. And it's not always as permanent as we'd like it to be. Another marvel of modern technology, spelled *hunk of junk*, that has little gaps in it. You see, sooner or later you'll go somewhere on a trip, or see someplace on TV, and you'll swear you've been there before, even though you know you never have been. Well, you were, when you went to one of our centers... That is, assuming you survive to go home.

"Now, stand still while I get the Transfer Extraction Dubulator set up. If you try to run, I'll just have to break your legs and carry you out to the car, and neither of us wants that."

Emil stood shaking as Ms. Gilman reached in the secretary's desk and took out what looked exactly like a small cassette tape recorder. She pulled a cord out of her purse that had a miniature plug-in jack on one end; the other end was connected to a small black penlight.

"I'll have to take a reading first," Ms. Gilman said. She held the penlight up and pointed it at Emil's forehead, then she took the jack on the other end, reached around to the back of her head, and plugged it into the base of her skull. The pupils in her eyes grew tiny, and Emil could see the veins in her neck and forehead standing out, like someone was strangling her. Then she pulled the little jack free. The veins shrank, and her eyes returned to normal.

"Good," she said, in a low, deep voice that reminded Emil of a movie reel running too slow. She cleared her throat loudly, and Emil could hear the sound change pitch, going back up again. "Very good." She pushed the plug into a jack on the side of the tape machine, then grinned. "And we're ready."

Just then, someone knocked at the door.

"Hello," Emil heard his own voice say from the other side of the whitish glass.

"Ah, he's here already," Ms Gilman said. She put the light down and went to open the door.

Emil did the only thing that made sense. He reached out and pulled the lever for the fire alarm.

Ms. Gilman jumped as the bell sounded, loud and jarring, from everywhere at once. She howled, then turned and lunged for the alarm lever, trying to shut it off.

Emil leaped toward the desk and snatched up the penlight. The machine it was attached to really did look just like an ordinary tape recorder. He didn't have many options. He could only think of one. As the alarm went silent he grabbed the penlight, pointed it as Ms. Gilman, and pushed RECORD.

Ms. Gilman started toward him but froze in midstride. The tape player ran for just a moment, then the button snapped up, shutting the machine off.

"Information ready for transfer," a thin, electronic voice said from the speaker on the tape machine.

Ms. Gilman just stood there, staring, as if she were in a trance. Emil didn't think it would last very long. He thought about what she had told him. You had to have the codes. There was no other way. He looked into the bright bulb of the penlight and pressed PLAY. Then everything went dark.

A moment later the light returned. Emil blinked, letting his head clear. He couldn't help but smile. He picked up the phone and punched in twenty digits. He waited a moment, then punched in four more digits and hung up. When he turned around Ms. Gilman was still standing there. It was going to be tough matching wits with her, once she recovered. Plenty to worry about; but he decided there just wasn't time to worry about it right now. He didn't want to be here when she came to.

He used Ms. Gilman's key to open the office door. Another Emil stood there quietly, eyes fixed, as if he weren't seeing anything at all.

Emil led his double down the hallway and out into the gloom. "Tell them Ms. Gilman sent you," he said, pointing his double toward the car.

Then Emil turned and walked toward his bike. The sun was coming up, the sky was clearing. Nothing to it, really, once you knew how: There were a lot of things he was going to change, he told himself, thinking about his mother and father first of all—but that bike was definitely one of them.

He got on and headed home.

CYPRESS SWAMP GRANNY

Marietta sat on the veranda
fanning herself, because there's
nothing hotter and stickier
than August in New Orleans,
and indoors wouldn't even be
bearable till evening. "The
trouble is," she complained,
"all the best boys went off to
that stupid war, and what
came back was worse than
what stayed."

"Hush!" Mama gave a
frantic look to Papa, snoring
one chair over; for Papa was

one of those who had gone, and he had lost a foot to an artillery barrage at the first battle of Bull Run.

Marietta waved her fan dismissively. It was one thing for Papa to have to walk with a cane. It was quite another matter to have boys Marietta was supposed to *dance* with come back from the war with arms and legs missing, or with awful scars, or—worst yet—like Billy Renfrew, who looked as fine as ever but now just sat there, his eyes focused on something nobody else could see; and occasionally his mother had to get out a handkerchief and wipe the drool from his chin.

"It just isn't fair," Marietta insisted.

"I swear"—Mama leaned back in her chair—"sometimes you're the most heartless child I know."

"Seventeen is not a child," said Marietta. "And all I'm saying is, it's a sad day when Louisa Beth Eldridge's family is giving a ball in one week's time, and the most eligible bachelor around is Will Stottle, with his too-narrow shoulders and his too-wide behind."

Mama patted Marietta's arm sympathetically. "Not," Mama pointed out, "of course, that Will Stottle is eligible anymore. He and your cousin Violet *have* formalized their engagement."

"Oh, Mother!" Marietta cried in exasperation. She shoved back her chair, with a scraping of wood on wood.

—just as young Ceecee, carrying a tray with glasses of tea, eased open the front door.

The chair hit the door, the door hit the tray—and tray, pitcher, and glasses crashed to the floor.

Mama cried out, brushing at the hem of her gown.

Papa snorted in his sleep but didn't wake up.

Ceecee, eight years old and unsure whether to curtsy and apologize first, or cry, or pick up the broken glass, or mop up the spreading puddle of tea, bobbed and wavered, trying to accomplish all at once.

Marietta fought the inclination to kick her, lest some bleeding-heart Yankee reconstructionist complain that they were mistreating the black help who had chosen to remain—at a *salary*, no less. Would anyone have believed such a thing just a few years back?

"This is unbearable!" Marietta cried, sweeping past Ceecee, who'd crouched to clean up the mess she had made. Ceecee leaned back to avoid the swing of Marietta's hem, lost her balance, and sat down heavily in the wetness.

Marietta ran down the veranda stairs and across the front lawn. At the very first, the breeze of running blew her hair off her face, which felt good. But after a short distance her clothes were clinging to her as though she had taken them damp off the line. She stopped running but didn't turn back.

The war hadn't ruined the DuChamps family, as it had ruined so many others. Their property had more or less survived intact—excepting the loss of the slaves, of course. But time was they could afford to go someplace cool for August, and that was certainly one more change for the worse.

On the hard-worn dirt path that led down to the river road, Marietta heard the light pitter-pat of Ceecee's bare feet.

"Missus says to go with you," Ceecee said. "See you don't get into trouble."

"Trouble?" Marietta shouted, though Mama would have said shouting wasn't refined. "*Trouble?* There's nothing to *do*."

"When I don't have nothing special to do," Ceecee said, "or when I'm troubled, I go visit my granny Orilla."

Marietta continued walking, though she had no destination in mind. Paris would have been nice. Natchez acceptable.

Ceecee came skipping after her. "Granny Orilla knows cures and curses—all kinds of spells—and she knows dreams—"

Marietta stopped so quickly that Ceecee almost collided with her. "What are you talking about?" she demanded.

"When my sister was afraid that her man was going to leave her, Granny Orilla gave her a root to put under his pillow, and he hasn't gone wandering since."

"A *root?*" Marietta repeated scornfully.

"White folk come to her, too, sometime," Ceecee said. "Remember how hard Missus Nattie wanted a baby, and she couldn't have none? Granny made a remedy for her she had to rub on her belly every night for six nights, and the seventh night she drank down what was left, and before the hibiscus bloomed—"

"Quiet," Marietta commanded, for everyone knew Nathalie Nye had had twin boys last year, after years of trying. "Where is this granny of yours?" she asked, for she had nothing better to do.

"Lives down by the cypress swamp," Ceecee said.

82

"Of course she does." Marietta sighed. "Lead the way."

The closer Marietta and Ceecee got to the swamp, the louder the insects whined and buzzed, sounding fierce enough to carry off small children. Granny Orilla's shack was nestled among moss-draped oaks.

"Granny Orilla!" Ceecee hollered shrilly, startling the chickens out from under the porch. "Granny Orilla!"

The old, skinny woman who came out of the cabin, leaning heavily on a hickory stick cane, was Creole—a mix: Most likely her daddy had been a plantation owner with an eye for the pretty slaves. This woman was not pretty, or at least she hadn't been in ages. Her hair—what she had left—was perfectly white.

"Ceecee, honey!" she crowed.

Ugly old thing, Marietta thought as girl and woman hugged.

"This is Miss Marietta," Ceecee said, "come to see you."

"How kind of you to visit," the woman Orilla said, too polite—sarcastic, even—as though she had read Marietta's thoughts on her face.

Ceecee dragged on her grandmother's arm, bringing her closer. "I was telling her about things you done, like for Missus Nattie," Ceecee said, "and she wanted to meet you."

Quick, before Marietta knew what was happening, Orilla laid her hand on Marietta's belly. "No luck making babies?" she asked.

Marietta slapped the bony hand away. "Uppity old

83

witch," she said. "Time was, I could have had you whipped for your insolence."

Orilla smiled a swamp creature's smile. "Times change," she answered.

Trying to make peace, Ceecee told Orilla, "She don't need help with babies. She don't even have a man."

Orilla continued to smile, as though the fault lay somehow with *Marietta* rather than with the war taking all the best boys away. "You looking to win one man special," she asked, "or any man?"

Marietta opened her mouth to protest, but then realized that *was* why she'd come. "Will Stottle," she answered.

She was aware of Ceecee gaping at her. "But that's Miss Violet's beau," the child said.

Orilla's dark eyes shifted from Marietta to Ceecee, back to Marietta.

"Will Stottle," Marietta repeated. "Ceecee says you've got some sort of root, or something?"

The smile widened. Orilla's teeth were yellow from age and looked too big for her shrunken, wrinkled face, giving her a slightly horsy appearance, though Marietta estimated there was more of crocodile than horse in Orilla's smile. "Oh, there's roots and there's herbs," the old woman said, "each with its own purpose. Let me see your hand."

She ran her callused finger along the lines that crossed Marietta's palm. "*Mmm-mmm-mmmm,*" she said, shaking her head disapprovingly.

Marietta snatched her hand away.

Orilla made her eyes go all wide and spooky. "I see you burning bright with the fire of passion," she said.

"I see you driving that poor boy mad with the wanting of you."

"But only with your help?" Marietta guessed, smirking.

Orilla let her eyes return to normal. "Girl like you should be satisfied with what you got. You should enjoy the sweet life the Lord give you while you can."

"I don't want your *advice*," Marietta said. "I want one of your potions. Or a root. Or an herb." She gave her own crocodile smile. "Or can't you do it?"

"There's a price," Orilla told her. "I'll require a year from your life."

"You expect *me* to work for *you* for a year? For Will *Stottle*?"

"Nothing to do with work, honey," Orilla said. "Not a year of your time. A year of your life. I'll take it off the end, where you're least likely to miss it, to add on to mine."

"Crazy old witch," Marietta said. "How, exactly, do you plan to collect this year?"

"By taking your hand, and you wishing it onto me."

Marietta looked at Ceecee, wondering what the catch was, what the two of them were up to. But she couldn't read anything on Ceecee's face. "Taken a lot of years from people, have you?" Marietta asked, flipping her hand, palm up, practically in Orilla's face. Orilla looked seventy or eighty.

"Oh, no." Orilla grinned. "This is something new I just learned." She rubbed a finger along the line that started between Marietta's thumb and forefinger and ran down to the wrist.

85

*Some*thing happened—a pain similar to hitting her elbow in just the wrong place.

Marietta snatched her hand back.

"Sorry," Orilla said. "Thank you." She had her hand clasped, as though to hold on tight to the year she seemed to believe she had taken.

What have I done? Marietta thought, suddenly afraid.

"It's only a year," Ceecee reassured her.

Marietta rubbed her hand, although, really, it had stopped hurting already. "What good's a year?" she taunted. Orilla *still* looked seventy or eighty.

"I can take this one year of yours"—Orilla held up her fist—"and stretch it out to ten years for me. Come." She gestured for Marietta to follow her into her cabin.

Which was probably as filthy as the slave shacks had ever been, and just as likely to fall down. "I'll wait here," Marietta said.

Orilla gave her awful smile, and she and Ceecee went indoors, leaving Marietta with the chickens.

Crazy old witch, Marietta thought again. Probably Orilla'd scratched her fingernail along Marietta's palm to cause that painful tingle, that old trickster. There was no mark, but Marietta found her cheeks burning at the thought of how frightened she'd momentarily been. A year, indeed!

But then the two of them came out, Ceecee skipping merrily, Orilla carrying a tiny burlap bag. "You sure this Will Stottle is the man you want?" Orilla asked. "Because this is a powerful remedy. And it only works the once."

"It only needs to work once," Marietta said. She didn't like the smile Orilla gave her at that.

"With the lights out and your eyes closed, go to sleep tonight thinking of your man," Orilla instructed. "Hold on to this here bag all night long. In the morning, you take the hand you held on to that bag with, and you make sure the first person you touch is him, skin to skin, without touching nobody in between."

Marietta sniffed the bag. Nothing foul, in any case. "Come along, Ceecee," she said, and headed back home without a thank-you or good-bye.

The next afternoon, Marietta paid a call on her cousin Violet. As she'd expected, Will Stottle was there.

Marietta kissed Violet's cheek. "Being in love suits you," she told Violet, not meaning a word of it. "You look lovely."

She let the old swamp granny's burlap bag drop from her hand into the silk purse that dangled from the same wrist. *All night long,* the old witch had said. Marietta had held the bag all morning, too, just to make sure. She clasped Will's hand in both of hers. "And, my, don't you look dashing! You make such a handsome couple."

"Well, thank you," Will said, not letting go of her hand.

In his eyes, Marietta saw a flicker of something that could have been a moment's surprise.

It worked, she thought in amazement, as Will continued to hold her hands and stare and stare as though he couldn't get enough of her. She hadn't quite believed it *could,* but Will was obviously having trouble remembering how to breathe.

"Well," Violet said in a fluttery voice after several—long—moments of the two of them looking deeply into each other's eyes, "how kind of you to visit, Marietta." She linked her arm around Will's, and he never even glanced at her.

"I came to let you know," Marietta said in a breathy voice, still gazing wistfully at Will, "if there's anything at all you want, you should be sure to just ask."

"Isn't that sweet?" Violet said. Good natured as a lop-eared pup, and about as intelligent, even she could see that something was wrong. "Thank you," she said. "You're very kind." Then: "Will, I'm sure Marietta has other errands to run today, and we really shouldn't keep her any longer." She shook his arm. *"Will."*

Marietta finally pulled her hands from Will's, first the left, then the right, that which had held Orilla's bag. She said, "You must come to visit me."

"Yes," Will agreed, on a long, drawn-out sigh.

"Yes," Violet said, much more shortly.

Outside, Marietta had just barely gotten her sun parasol up when Will burst out of the door. "May I join you?" he called after her.

Marietta smiled, knowing she'd won.

Whether the problem was that Will Stottle wasn't a man of strong character to begin with, or that Marietta had held on to Granny Orilla's magical remedy bag too long, Will's single-minded devotion quickly plummeted from flattering to annoying to embarrassing to downright burdensome. He was always there. Always. At her side. Trying to take hold of her elbow. Protesting his undying love.

The night of the Eldridges' ball, Marietta was relieved that Louisa Beth's family had banned Will Stottle because of the scandalous way he had behaved toward Violet.

"Who is that gorgeous man?" she asked Louisa Beth, spying across the room a man who had broad shoulders and a fine behind.

"Daniel Clarke," Louisa Beth said. "He's a business acquaintance of Daddy's. He is—you will kindly pardon the expression—a Yankee—but he's quite charming in spite of it. He's not only handsome, he's almost shamefully rich." Louisa Beth struck her playfully with her fan. "I'll introduce you if you promise not to drive him to distraction, the way you did with poor Will."

Marietta laughed innocently. She had threatened to beat Ceecee senseless—emancipation or not—if she ever said anything about her going to visit Granny Orilla. Everyone assumed the fault was Will's. And it *was* Will's fault, Marietta reasoned. It was one thing to love someone. It was quite another to act the fool.

She followed Louisa Beth around the fringe of the dancing. Close up, the Yankee looked even better than he had from across the room.

"Miss Marietta DuChamps," Louisa Beth said, "may I please present Mr. Daniel Clarke of Pennsylvania. Don't let his youth fool you, Marietta, my dear. Mr. Clarke is a leader of industry *and* banking who now wants to expand his sphere of influence to farming, too."

"How fascinating," Marietta purred, fluttering her eyelashes.

But try as hard as she could to give the impression that she hung on his every word, that she lived only to hear him speak, after a few polite pleasantries, Daniel Clarke let himself get distracted by somebody's mother.

Marietta tried again later that night, when everybody went outside to enjoy the cool of the garden. She even managed to sit down next to him, though she practically had to knock Louisa Beth off the bench. But she could tell he'd already forgotten meeting her, not two hours earlier. Before she could reacquaint him with herself, Will Stottle came crashing through the bougainvillea, begging to be allowed to sit at her feet.

It was obviously time to go home.

The next morning, Marietta had Ceecee once more lead her to Granny Orilla's cabin in the cypress swamp.

They found Orilla crawling out from under the porch, gathering the chickens' eggs into a basket. She didn't have her cane with her—not that it would have been much use under the porch.

Did she look younger? Orilla wore a kerchief today, which hid her hair, so Marietta couldn't be sure. Slaves looked old fast, backs bending under constant labor, faces creased by worry. Emancipation didn't cure that. Though Orilla's magic had obviously worked with Will, this business of taking away a year and changing it to ten was harder to believe.

"So, Missy," Orilla greeted her. "How'd my remedy work?"

"Not very well," Marietta said.

"Too well," Ceecee corrected, and knew enough to duck.

"Will Stottle is making a nuisance of himself," Marietta explained. "He won't be put off."

"Week after a love remedy?" Orilla snorted. "I should hope not."

"Make me up a new bag," Marietta said. "Not quite so strong. For a different man, by the name of Daniel Clarke."

Orilla shook her head. "Won't work. I *told* you that. Love remedy only works but the once. Be happy with what you got, sugar. Take things one at a time, each in its own time. No need you have to have a man this very instant."

"I'm willing to pay," Marietta insisted. She'd never heard of somebody refusing to be paid.

But Orilla was still shaking her head.

"If you can't sell me another love potion, sell me something else."

"Like what?" Orilla asked.

Marietta remembered seeing Daniel Clarke talking and laughing with Louisa Beth Eldridge and with Daphne Winslowe and with Dolores Montac. "Make me beautiful."

"All seventeen-year-olds is beautiful," Orilla said. Then, with unexpected kindness, she added, "You're a fine-looking girl."

"I want hair the same golden color as Louisa Beth's. And I want a long, straight nose like Daphne's, and a teeny-tiny waist like Dolores's."

"Those aren't things that matter at all," Orilla said, but she stepped forward. "Hardly worth a year."

91

Marietta held out her hand.

Shaking her head, no longer giving her swamp-creature smile, Orilla took Marietta's hand and ran a finger over the palm, causing another shiver of pain.

Afterward, she brought out another tiny burlap bag. "Tonight, steep this in a kettleful of hot water until the water boils down to one cupful. Then set the cup to cool where the moonlight is shining on it. Once it's cool enough, drink it all down without taking any breaths in between. And all the while you're drinking, you think on the features you be wanting."

Marietta snatched the bag away, disappointed that she had to wait until the night. "Come, Ceecee," she said.

Still, the bag was a success. By morning, Marietta's hair had lengthened, lightened, thickened, and curled. Her waist curved in nice and tight, and her breasts curved out, and her nose was straight and narrow.

She told her mother—who interrupted to say she looked especially lovely that morning—that she needed to go to Oakridge to thank the Eldridges for the delightful time she'd had at the ball. She didn't mention that she hoped to interrupt the Eldridge family—including their houseguest, Mr. Daniel Clarke—at their breakfast.

Papa rode with her in case Will Stottle should be loitering about the river road, which he was. Papa gave him a stern talking-to, which Marietta guessed did no good at all.

At Oakridge the Eldridges invited Marietta and Papa to join them for breakfast on the veranda. Marietta even managed to squeeze herself between Daniel and

Louisa Beth. Louisa Beth's mother—bless her soul!—commented on how Marietta's gown really suited her figure, and how the color brought out the golden highlights in her hair.

"A beauty," Mr. Eldridge agreed, as Marietta ducked her head shyly, so that her hair would catch the sparkle of the early morning sun. "It's no wonder young Will Stottle is besotted of her."

"Ah," Daniel said, "the young man who had to be forcefully ejected from the ball." He looked at her, Marietta thought, with new appreciation.

"The boy is such a fool," she said.

Daniel raised his eyebrows coolly. "It's difficult to be so young, and so in love."

"Surely, sir," Marietta protested, "you don't excuse his bad manners?"

"I don't excuse anyone's bad manners," Daniel answered. "I simply point out that youthful exuberance is sometimes its own punishment."

"Yes," Louisa Beth said, so solemnly that everyone laughed, and Louisa Beth blushed prettily.

Marietta pouted and plotted.

"The problem is," Marietta told Orilla—who was gray haired but definitely younger than last time—"the Eldridges are rich, and we're only well off."

"A man who cares that much for money," Orilla said, "ain't worth having."

"That's none of your business," Marietta snapped.

" 'Course it ain't." Orilla was wearing that crocodile smile of hers again. Her teeth gleamed white and strong.

Marietta had found her own way this time, and she

was glad Ceecee wasn't here to pick up any of her grandmother's sass.

Orilla, who'd been scrabbling around in her herb garden, wiped her hands on her apron. "Make-money remedies are dangerous," she warned. "A love remedy, a beauty remedy—that's just giving what's already there a nudge. *Money*'s got to come from somewhere. Can't say for certain"—Orilla shook her head—"but lots of time, money comes from somebody else's misfortune—'specially money that comes fast, like you want it." When Marietta didn't answer, she added, "Like maybe somebody dying."

"Are you saying my parents might die?" Marietta asked.

"Not if I make the spell be for money coming into your house," Orilla said. "But other people."

"Then do it." Marietta held her hand out.

"Such a sweet child," Orilla said.

Burying Orilla's bag at midnight was worth the blisters, and the worry she caused Papa—who was sure that moles had invaded the front walk during the night—for the very next morning, as they left Saint Louis Cathedral after mass, a young boy came up to them carrying a big, thick envelope. "Message for Miss Marietta DuChamps from Mr. Will Stottle," the boy announced.

Her parents groaned.

People around them tittered.

But there was no sign of Will, and Orilla had said that bespelled money could come from unexpected directions, so Marietta took the envelope. There was a letter.

My dearest Marietta, my love, my reason for living, awakener of my soul, enkindler of my heart, my truest—

Marietta started skipping words and phrases, aware that the church crowd had not dispersed but was discreetly waiting in the square to see what this was all about. On the third page, the words "offered to you" caught Marietta's eye.

I offered to you my heart, but you would not have it.

She started to skip forward, but then came back.

I offered to you my heart, but you would not have it. Accept, then, my heart's blood. For Grandfather always said that earth was the heart's blood of the Stottles. That was why we left England, to have our own land. So now I offer to you Wellhaven Plantation—my home, my property, my heart's blood. I do not offer this as a lure to entice you to my side, but as a gift, freely given, for I am no longer happy there, since I am without you. Accept it, with or without me. The marble halls hold no more charm for me, the rich delta soil—

It started to get sentimental, and Marietta lost patience. She turned to the last page. It was the deed to Wellhaven, signed over to her, granting her all rights and monies, now and forever.

"Oh, my," she said, fanning herself.

She spotted Daniel Clarke standing with the Eldridges. She spoke up loudly and clearly, as befitted the mistress of a plantation. "Will Stottle has just given me Wellhaven, as a token of his affection."

There was a murmur of surprise, sounding— Marietta realized after a long moment of smiling sweetly—more shocked than pleased.

"You can't possibly be thinking of accepting this offer?" said Mr. Eldridge.

Marietta looked down her long, perfect nose at him. "Why not?"

"Because the poor boy's wits are obviously addled. Possibly the effect of the horrors he witnessed in the war, and of coming back to find his father dead and his mother dying."

"And *my* effect on him," Marietta reminded, standing straight to emphasize her bosom.

Next to her, Mama said softly, disapprovingly, "It wouldn't be proper."

"Yes, it would." Marietta was shocked at the unexpected *attack* from her mother. She looked to Papa for support. "This will more than double our property," she reminded him.

But Papa, wearing a stern look, only shook his head, tight lipped.

"Well, he didn't give it to *you*," Marietta said, "he gave it to *me*. Which makes *me* wealthier than *you*."

She tossed her head to make her golden hair sparkle in the sunshine.

And she caught sight of Daniel Clarke, who wore exactly the same expression Papa did.

What was the matter with everyone? She was young, and beautiful, and rich. Just the kind of person everybody loved.

But suddenly Will Stottle was there. His clothes were all wrinkled as though he'd slept in them, and his eyes were too bright, and he was smiling at her, looking much like a slave trying to escape a beating by acting all hopeful and meek. "Is it enough, Marietta?" he asked. "Is it enough to make you love me?"

They were all pitying him, she realized. *He* was making *her* look bad in Daniel Clarke's eyes.

"Love you?" She practically spit. "Will Stottle, I despise you. I'd give anything to be rid of you."

She heard the collective gasp of those gathered in the square.

It didn't matter. She knew what she had to do.

"Girl, you back again?" Granny Orilla jumped off the upended crate on which she'd been standing to fix her cabin's tarpaper roof. Her hair was black and shiny, and she looked not quite as old as Marietta's mother, possibly thirty-five or -six years old. "I swear I never met nobody so dissatisfied with everything."

"Will Stottle is ruining my life," Marietta said.

"You don't know nothing about ruined lives," Orilla told her.

"Take another year"—Marietta held out her hand —"and make him stop loving me."

97

"I see you burning bright with the fire of passion," Orilla said. It took a moment for Marietta to realize the old witch was repeating the same words she had said that first day.

"Not for Will!" Marietta shouted. "I can't live this way!"

Orilla sighed. "No, I suppose you can't." She took Marietta's hand. "The taking away of love," she said, "is a chancy thing. There's no telling—"

"Yes, yes," Marietta said. "Just do it."

Orilla did it.

That night Marietta awoke with Will Stottle's hand over her mouth.

He must have climbed the cherry tree and gotten in through her window, for in the moonlight she could see where his foot had come down on the curtain, ripping it from the rod.

Maybe Papa had heard him entering, she thought, and was even now coming down the hall to see what was the matter.

But she was in the very room, and *she* hadn't heard.

"Where is it?" Will hissed into her ear.

Leave it to Will to cover someone's mouth, then start asking questions.

Marietta made a move to swat his hand away, because he was beginning to hurt her, but he showed his other hand, the one that wasn't over her mouth: He had a knife.

She was frightened, a bit—but mostly she was very, very angry.

"Softly, now," he whispered, and slowly took his hand away from her mouth. "Where's the deed?"

"Changed your mind?" she asked softly but scornfully. "I thought I was the love of your life, your reason for being. I thought you gave me Wellhaven, whether I'd have you or not?"

"I don't know what possessed me," Will said. "I never cared for you. I need to see if Violet will have me back."

"After the spectacle you've made of yourself?" Marietta asked from between clenched teeth. "You'll never be able to show your face without everybody laughing. You'd best try to start new someplace else."

"Wellhaven is *my* land," Will said. "My grand-daddy—"

"The deed's in the nightstand drawer." Marietta pointed. "But everybody *knows* you gave it to me. Everybody *knows* I'd never give it back unless you threatened me. Think that's the kind of man Violet wants? One who shames her and breaks his word and threatens women?"

For a moment Marietta feared she'd gone too far. Will stood looming over her bed, and she realized that he *might* kill her. He might not be satisfied with retrieving the deed.

But then he opened the drawer she had pointed out. Should she try to escape, calling for help? He was only two steps away, and she didn't dare, knowing that might be the action to tip the balance. A moment later, he slipped his knife away. She heard the scrape of a match, and the oil lamp on her nightstand flared to life.

"It's the deed," she assured him, thinking that he suspected some trick, "the same deed you gave me."

"You're right," he said, and it took her a moment to realize he was answering what she'd said before, not what she'd just said. "It could never be the same."

Then he put the parchment to the flame.

"You fool!" she cried out.

With his free hand, he shoved her back down, then he dropped the burning paper onto her bed. "Yes," he agreed. He swung the lamp, flinging burning oil over the furniture, the floor, the bedcovers. And still he held her down, preventing her from scrambling away from the rapidly spreading fire.

"Papa!" Marietta screamed, but already the air shimmered from the heat, and already it was hard to breathe.

Will just sat there, holding her tight.

As the paddle wheeler went up the river, the passengers caught a glimpse of the burned-out shell that had been the DuChamps family home for three generations. Daniel Clarke shook his head at the terrible waste.

But then he turned his attention back to the charming and beautiful young Creole woman. "Much more opportunity in the North," he assured her, finishing the thought he'd started. "I'm sure you and your..." He hesitated, unsure—she was obviously too young to be the child's mother. "Sister?" he asked.

"Ceecee's closer to being my niece."

"I'm sure you and your niece will love Philadelphia," Daniel finished. He hesitated, not wanting to sound too forward, since they'd only just met. "But if

100

you don't know anyone in Philadelphia, I'd welcome the opportunity to be your guide."

"How kind of you," Ceecee's aunt said. "May I repay you by telling your fortune?" She took his hand, then looked up, her dark eyes pleased and friendly. "Look"—she showed him where—"a nice, strong, *long* lifeline."

JOY OESTREICHER

FAMILY PLANNING

The third time Cory walked
Maggie Smith home, he
thought for sure she was going
to let him kiss her. She talked
to him the whole way. They
stopped and looked at Gert's
trout pond together. He took
her hand as they crossed the
footbridge over the highway,
and she didn't let go even
when they walked up the long
dusty driveway to her house.

They stood together outside
her door. He could see into the

window by the porch. A pale slender hand held back the curtain. Someone was watching them.

"My sister," Maggie said, without looking. She seemed friendlier today, as if he'd passed some kind of test. "Well, see you tomorrow, OK?" Her long honey-amber hair swung off her shoulder when she tilted her head.

"Yeah." Cory dared to reach out and brush back a few fine strands of hair that had blown into her violet eyes. She smiled at him and he began to lean forward, ready to put his lips against hers.

He kissed air as she abruptly turned away. Cory just stood there like a fool as she opened her door, went through, and shut it with barely a sound. He could see her through the curtain as she waved good-bye from inside the house.

Was she in the kitchen now? Cory didn't know what part of the house she'd gone into. She had never let him inside the house. Yet. He scowled.

Tom Madsen, who had *thousands* of girlfriends, had told him, "You have to get 'em to invite you in. The kitchen's best. Nice and homey and family-like, where they feel safe. And then..."

And then Cory walked home alone again.

On Friday, Maggie actually came and found him during lunch break. They sat on the grass and ate together. Cory was really looking forward to walking her home. He was surprised to realize he felt sorry the weekend was coming. Usually Saturday and Sunday were great; Dad worked weekends, so Cory had the time to himself. He could shoot some hoops, watch the tube—cartoons, or MTV, maybe, or movies from Dad's private collection. Have anything he wanted to eat. Play video games.

But this week, it meant he wouldn't see Maggie again until Monday. Well, one thing at a time. It was Friday, and on Friday he could walk her home from school one more time.

The dirt in the driveway seemed thicker and dustier than ever in the hot, still air. "Are these your pastures?" Cory asked.

Maggie looked around them, as if surprised to see the brown weed-choked fields. "Yeah, I guess. We used to have horses, but Mother had to sell them."

"Too bad," Cory said. He grinned at her. "We could go riding."

Maggie's smile was quick, then gone. "Oh, we don't go outdoors much. Mother's not well, so we mostly stay home."

It was hard not to stare at her as they climbed the hill. Her legs moved steadily beneath the delicate material of her violet dress. It matched her eyes. He glanced at her sideways from time to time, admiring the way she moved. She was so pretty. He could hardly believe she was interested in him.

They neared the top of the hill. A few ancient oaks hung their heavy branches over the driveway. Without even talking about it, Cory and Maggie stopped and stood in the shade. The huge old Victorian farmhouse sat like a crown on the hill's head, its many roof peaks and windows decorated with wooden lattices and balls and spindles, like Cory was learning to make on the lathe in wood shop.

"Have I ever met your sister?" he wondered, thinking about the hand that had held back the curtain.

"Which one?"

"You have more than one?"

"Kate, Becca, Toralee, and Amanda all live at home," Maggie said. She glanced at him. "Susanna is the oldest. She has her own house over in Glen Ellen. I'm the youngest."

"I guess I never heard of them at school, or anything," Cory said. Which was weird, when he thought of it. Five older sisters, and he'd never heard of them? The Smiths weren't new to the area; his dad would have known if they'd bought in recently. Yountville was still small enough that people knew who their neighbors were. The Smiths had lived in that house ... a long time.

"They're all a lot older than me," Maggie explained. At his blank look, Maggie laughed. "My sisters are," she reminded him.

"Oh. Could I—"

"Would you like to come in?"

"Yeah. Sure, I'd like that."

Maggie led the way around the side of the house. They walked through knee-deep dead grass and weeds to a door Cory hadn't seen before. It had to be the "front" door, since it was big and wooden, with fancy carvings. The window above the door was made of stained glass, gnomelike faces staring down at him. Their expressions made them seem like they knew something he didn't know, kind of smug and snotty looking.

Maggie opened the door and they went in. The room was dim and filled with furniture. A living room. Or maybe it was called a parlor in a house this old. Well, he wasn't in the kitchen yet, but if her mother and sisters were home, maybe it was just as well. Cory didn't think he could kiss her with an audience, even in the kitchen. He wasn't sure he could kiss her at all, but was desperate to try. Fifteen years old and never been kissed! If the guys at school knew, they'd razz him forever. He could feel his cheeks get hot, just thinking about it.

"Would you like some lemonade?"

Anything to stay longer. "Yes, please, that'd be great." Actually it did sound good. Cold and wet and a little sour. Refreshing, before he had to walk home.

"Andrew, would you get us some lemonade?" Maggie asked.

A man in his early twenties was suddenly standing in the front corner of the room. Cory hadn't seen him there a moment ago. It was kind of spooky how he suddenly appeared, his jeans new and fresh looking, his T-shirt white and smooth, like he'd just walked out of a closet. Except there wasn't any closet. Cory stared at the wall a moment, certain the guy hadn't been there when they'd walked in.

The man didn't speak, but gave Maggie a solemn nod and silently left the room, not making a sound in his black Adidas.

Maybe that's how he snuck in, Cory thought. *He walks like a ghost.* He turned back to face Maggie. "Uh, here's your backpack," he said, handing it to her by a strap.

"Thank you, Cory. Would you set it on the chaise lounge?" She met his eyes, and he was captivated a moment by how beautiful they were, deep and violet like the sky at dusk.

His arm started to ache from holding out the backpack; he came back to himself and looked around. "What's a—where did you say to put it?"

Maggie waved a hand toward a one-armed sofa thing. "There."

He set the backpack on the dark flowery fabric, then turned to Maggie. She was just sitting down on a padded bench in front of a long, polished table. She patted the place next to her, and he went and sat down, too, just as Andrew returned carrying a tray with two glasses of lemonade. He set a glass in front of each of them. *Just like in a restaurant*, Cory thought.

Then Cory and Maggie were alone in the big room. Andrew left the way he'd originally come, in silence, into nowhere. It bothered Cory, in the back of his mind, but he didn't want to solve mysteries now. He wanted Maggie to like him.

It was awful. He couldn't think of a thing to say. One hand held the lemonade glass; the other rather desperately picked at the side seam of his jeans. He sipped. "Good," he said stupidly.

Maggie raised her eyebrows.

"The lemonade. It's good."

She nodded. "Yes. Fargo makes it from scratch. He's very good with his hands." For no apparent reason Maggie blushed. "In the kitchen," she added.

Thoroughly confused, Cory said, "What?"

"Fargo is Kate's man. He's good in the kitchen; he's our cook."

"Oh." Evidently the house really had more than sisters in it. Maybe Andrew wasn't a ghost. "Andrew...?"

"He's Amanda's. Everyone made fun of them at first: Amanda and Andrew—and Amanda *won't* let anyone call her Mandy, so it sounds funny with all those *A*s. Or it used to. Now it sounds fine. You can get used to anything, I guess."

Cory mused on that awhile, drinking his lemonade.

"We shouldn't have been surprised," Maggie said. "Susanna chose Samson, and Amanda always admired her. Then Susanna started naming her kids with *S* names: Sarah, Sally, Shenandoa. Sounds like a snake factory, don't you think?"

"Uh, kind of."

"Becca is more like Kate, practical. Down to earth."

"And you?"

"Becca's man is Micah." She looked at him. "Me, we don't know about yet."

Cory nodded like he understood, but he wasn't sure he did. "Isn't there another sister?"

"Toralee." Maggie seemed uncomfortable.

Cory looked at her, interested.

"Toralee didn't listen to Mother when she chose Billy. We had a lot of trouble over that one. Billy doesn't fit in. It still hasn't been all worked out."

"So how many people live here?"

"Well, Kate has Lily and Trina, Becca has just Anne so far, and Amanda hasn't started yet, so that's six. But Toralee has Judith"—she counted them off on her fingers—"Carla, Mari, and Pam. And then there's

Mother. Six and six again, plus me, makes thirteen." She looked at Cory. "You can see why we don't like that number. Toralee should have waited."

"But what about Fargo and Andrew and...?"

"Yes, I suppose you could count them in, though they aren't Smiths. That would make seventeen. And Papa, but he hardly ever comes out anymore, so nobody would count him."

There was a strangeness about it, but Cory couldn't put his finger on what, exactly, didn't add up. He finished his lemonade, then Maggie escorted him to the door. Her violet eyes were wide, her cheeks smooth and kissable.

"See you Monday, then," Cory said. Something about the wall where Andrew had appeared bothered him. Thinking about Andrew, Cory began to imagine he saw the guy right there, like a fresco on the wall.

"Oh, Cory...?" Maggie said.

Cory blinked and looked at her.

She smiled and went on, "Would you come over on Sunday? We have our big family brunch then, and you could meet everyone."

Startled, Cory fumbled a moment before he could say, "Uh, yeah, I guess so. That would be fine." A chance to see Maggie again before Monday? It would be better than fine.

"Good. Would you please plan to be here by one o'clock sharp? Mother hates it when we have to wait for someone who's late."

"Certainly." Cory found himself bending over in a little bow, feeling like an idiot at his impulse; but Maggie seemed to think it was charming.

She smiled at him, tilted her head, and said, "I'll see you Sunday, then."

On his way home, Cory couldn't stop thinking about her. It was kind of weird, all those people living together in one house, but then the house was certainly big enough.

Then again, with all those guys living there, you'd think someone would clean up the yard and fields. They had milkweed three feet tall along one fence. Once that stuff got started, it was hard to get rid of.

Cory shook his head. What did he care about milkweed? The total of his experience with horses or anything else that might use a pasture was three rides on a friend's old mare.

Still, Maggie's fields seemed empty to him. They needed horses in them. And maybe some goats or a cow for milk.

For a town boy, Cory thought at himself, *you're certainly hot for pastures all of a sudden.* He grinned. It wasn't pastures he was interested in, it was Maggie. It was her violet eyes and sweet lips. He frowned. Well, he was sure they'd *be* sweet, if he ever got the chance to find out.

Sunday, noon. Cory dialed his father's office. "Roger Sanders, please," he said to the woman who answered the phone. When his father came on the line, Cory spoke quickly. "Hi, Dad. Sorry to bother you. Just wanted to tell you I'm going to Maggie Smith's house for lunch. I'll be home by the time you are." *Probably well before,* Cory thought.

He changed clothes again, finally deciding on jeans

and a soft knit shirt with a collar. He thought about Maggie's family as he cut some roses from his mother's sturdy plants in the backyard.

Girls, that was it. Maggie only had sisters. And all her little nieces and nephews were *nieces*. Wasn't that a little out of proportion? And Maggie didn't even think of any of her brothers-in-law as family, though they lived with her. She hadn't counted them as Smiths, anyway. Would she want to keep her name and not take his, then?

"Whoa, hang on!" When the devil had he decided to marry her? He hadn't even kissed her yet! Cory laughed at himself as he started his walk across town "Jeez. Who would have thought I'd be such a domestic type? Pastures, family, marriage. Jeez!"

Maybe because his own family was so small, he wanted . . . what? More people around? Security?

Cory felt a deep pang of loss. Three years ago his mother had been working in her beloved garden even though rain was threatening and the sky was dark with clouds. Lightning had struck her, and Cory had come home from school to a yard full of emergency vehicles and strangers who tried to comfort him. Their pity had only made it worse. His mother was dead, and nothing was going to bring her back.

Until he'd met Maggie, Cory had wanted to get away—from the yard, the house, the town. Everything reminded him of his mother. He tried to talk his dad into moving, but, "Roger Sanders is a name in real estate here, Cory. We can't leave." Roger Sanders had an agency of his own—he wasn't about to start all over somewhere new. So that was that.

It was his dad's way of getting away from the hurt. *He runs away from the memories by working all the time.*

Maybe that was why Cory couldn't get Maggie out of his thoughts. Well, he didn't *want* to think about other things.

He started up Maggie's long driveway. *Really, it's a road to her house, not a driveway. There ought to be a sign: SMITH ROAD. Some flowers along the fences.* From this angle, nearly halfway up the hill, he could just see the old barn. More and more of its peeling east wall appeared as he ascended. The house sat slightly to the right of the barn, looking freshly painted and in much better repair.

He checked his watch. Twenty minutes left. It would take him another five to get to the top of the hill, a couple more to cool off after the hot, dusty climb, and then what? Ring the bell? Maggie hadn't said anything about being early. He decided to stop under the next big oak and enjoy the shade, let a little time pass.

He rested a hand atop the post of the wobbly fence and stared out at the pasture. The milkweed challenged him. It needed to be hacked out at the roots and burned. He'd have to wear heavy gloves when he did it, so the thorny spines on the stems didn't tear up his hands. Maggie liked men who were good with their hands.

"Better get on up there," a voice said. A man's voice.

Cory whipped around. A guy about thirty was walking down the driveway, down toward town.

"Who are you?"

"Name's Fargo," he said.

"Kate's man," they said together.

Cory nodded at him.

"Got to go into town and pick up some things. I made fresh bread; if you get on up there now, it'll still be warm."

Cory nodded again. "Thank you. I'll do that."

Fargo walked on down the hill, so Cory turned and started up again. When he got to the top, Maggie was outside waiting for him.

"Hi," he said. She was wearing a white dress, her hair loose and curling across her shoulders. "You look pretty." Stupid, stupid. She was far more than pretty.

But Maggie smiled and tilted her head. "Thank you. Are those for me?"

Cory suddenly remembered the roses he'd cut. He gave her the bouquet, red and white and pink old-fashioned roses with a beautiful fresh scent. Maggie smelled them and smiled.

Thanks, Mom. She likes your roses.

"Would you come inside now? Everyone's ready to meet you."

Her family sat at the table where he and Maggie had drunk lemonade. It was longer now than it had been then—it had to be longer—there were what seemed to him dozens of women gathered around it. They all stared at him. It was like a laser attack, all those deep blue-violet gazes, and Cory felt totally stupid, ugly, clumsy, and poorly dressed—but only for a moment, because suddenly they all smiled. When they all smiled at him like that, Cory felt warm and welcome and a part of something important and happy.

"This is Mother," Maggie said, standing beside an older woman. Cory bowed to her, a tall, handsome lady with thick gray hair. She turned slightly to speak to Maggie. She was strong and regal and he wished she were his own mother. Whatever her mother said quietly into her ear, Maggie laughed, a throaty chuckle that made Cory shiver with pleasure. When the matriarch looked at him again, Cory saw echoes of Maggie in the deep, evening-sky eyes.

Someone said something; Cory heard his name. It brought him back to himself. He bowed again to Mother, then went to his place beside Maggie.

They ate and talked. He didn't say much, but he listened a lot.

"Is Cory going to stay with us?" a little golden-haired girl asked. She grinned like an imp at him as she handed him the bread. Cory grinned back.

The bread was warm and fresh, and very good. It needed butter worthy of it, though. Fresh churned, from a fat Guernsey cow, Cory decided.

Later, Maggie announced, "I'm showing him the house," and the other women at the table smiled and nodded to one another. Maggie stood up, and Cory followed her without question. He was curious about the big old house anyway, and the chance to be with Maggie alone was wonderful.

"They're a bit overwhelming at first, aren't they?"

It didn't sound like she expected an answer, so Cory just laughed as they climbed the stairs.

"Here's the babies' room." Sure enough, there were two small children in cribs, sound asleep. Cory thought they looked sweet, one with her little diaper-clad fanny sticking up in the air, thumb in her mouth. The other was perfect, with long, dark eyelashes that rested softly against her pink cheeks. "One thing about Billy," Maggie said. "He makes beautiful babies."

Cory flushed with embarrassment, but she didn't seem to notice. They moved on, Maggie showing him other children's rooms, bathrooms, hallways, sitting rooms, a playroom stuffed with toys "made by Micah. He's our builder." There was a room with nothing in it but a piano and a bare floor. "For dance, of course," Maggie said.

"Yes," Cory said. It seemed sensible, with this many girls.

The dance room was all of wood. The paneling on the walls and the hardwood floor seemed to hold pictures, the grain smooth and dark against the lighter background. Cory thought he saw a face or two, an old man and maybe a cat.

"Look," Maggie said. "These are our rooms," and by that she meant the sisters'. "Kate's." Sunny, with stout oak furnishings and a big oval rug on the floor. "Amanda's." Lots of pink and flounces and stuff. Becca's was blue and white. They passed a closed door.

Cory had automatically paused at it, expecting Maggie to open it, lead the way in.

"That's Toralee's," she said. She looked at him. "Billy's in there."

He started to walk onward with her, but then she stopped.

"No, you might as well see him now." She returned to the door and opened it.

Cory stepped in. It was like an Arabian Nights video in his father's collection. Dark wood walls. Hangings and fringe all done in deep reds and golds and black. It was kind of interesting. Different. Cory turned to walk out.

He saw Billy.

It had to be Billy, Cory supposed. There wasn't anyone else in here. Billy was in the wall. Or Billy *was* the wall.

"He doesn't come out very often. He gets wild sometimes," Maggie said. "It's a shame, but Mother *told* Toralee not to choose him, and there you are."

Billy's face and body seemed molded from wood. He was a good-looking young man; Cory could see why Toralee had been tempted against Mother's advice. Billy's mouth was open as if he would yell. His hands reached out with rigid intensity, reminding Cory of a statue he'd seen in an old movie.

Cory stared at him in disapproval. "You're right not to let him come out," he said, suddenly certain of it. "He'd get more than wild."

Maggie's room was violet and cream. It smelled of lavender. She didn't have to tell him it was hers; it fit her perfectly. She reached her hand up and brushed his cheek. "Would you let me choose you?" she whispered.

Inside him, where she couldn't see it, a flame of resistance rose up. This wasn't how he'd planned to live.

No, he'd go home to an empty room in an empty house. He'd finish school, and go on to college, and to an empty career where he'd hide all his thoughts and feelings. Or ... He thought of the Smiths all smiling at him, and the warmth of belonging made him smile, too. All resistance flickered and died.

He met Maggie's violet eyes. Would he let her choose him? Dumbly, Cory nodded.

Downstairs, she showed him the kitchen. Cory didn't even dream of trying to kiss her.

Out back, she waved her arm wide. "This is your place," she said. "The tack room, the barn and stable and fields—all yours." When she looked at him, her smile was radiant. "It will be nice to have horses again."

The ceremony was held at the Smiths' house. It was old-fashioned in style, like the heirloom dress Maggie wore.

When Roger Sanders came looking for Cory a few weeks later, he didn't think to look in the barn. He never even got that far.

"He's not around today," Becca Smith said at the front door. "He's such a hard worker, we're giving him a holiday."

"He should be in school."

"Cory doesn't need school to be happy here, Mr. Sanders."

Roger Sanders came back several times, but Cory was never there.

The horses were, though. And the yard and fields were looking better and better. The pastures were green and weed free. The dusty road up to the Smiths' house was brightened with flowers along its edge, which the goats kept trying to reach through the strong, fine fence. A tan-and-white cow chewed its cud beneath one of the old oaks.

Even the long driveway had improved. It had become less rough and dusty, and was marked with a neatly lettered sign that said SMITH ROAD.

The last time he came, Mr. Sanders forgot to ask about Cory altogether. As Maggie walked him out to the road, they were joined by another young woman, and another, and two more. They all stared at him with their lovely violet eyes, and Mr. Sanders forgot why he came.

"Do you want to sell your house?" he asked.

"No, we're happy here," Maggie said.

From his comfortable place in the new barn wall, Cory watched the man go away.

BRUCE COVILLE

THE JAPANESE MIRROR

I was bleeding the first time I saw the Japanese mirror. I had been cleaning the side counter in Mr. Colella's Curio Shoppe, and an unexpected piece of metal had sliced open my fingertip.

Crying out in rage, I threw my rag to the counter, stuck my bleeding finger into my mouth, and stamped my foot. I probably would have stamped again, except I noticed Mr. Colella giving me a warning stare.

I took a deep breath and tried to get my temper under control. I knew I might lose my job if I didn't watch myself, and I didn't want that to happen. Not only did I really need the money, I actually liked working with the strange junk the old man kept in his antique shop.

I took my finger from my mouth to look at the cut. It went straight across my fingertip. And it hurt like crazy. All those nerves so close to the surface, I guess.

Scanning the countertop, I found what had snagged me—the top of a screw Mr. Colella had used to make a repair and hadn't wound deeply enough into the wood.

I was still hunting for a Band-Aid when Mr. Colella shouted, "Jonathan, come here. I need your help."

Pressing thumb against fingertip to stem the bleeding, I went to the back room.

Mr. Colella was standing in front of a large wooden crate. "Open this," he said, handing me a crowbar. *"Gently."*

The mirror inside the crate—a Japanese mirror, according to Mr. Colella—was nearly eight feet tall. The glass was surrounded by a wooden frame carved with interlocking designs and finished in black lacquer. I couldn't help but imagine strange messages hidden among those whorling symbols. Though the silvering behind the glass had worn thin in two or three places, for the most part the reflection it gave was clean and pure.

"Not bad, eh?" said Mr. Colella, once I had all the packing pulled away. He pulled at the ends of his gray mustache, always a sign that he was pleased with an item.

"What do you think you'll get for it?" I asked.

He shrugged. "It's in good condition; it's a little unusual. Given its age, it could go for maybe three thousand. Maybe a little more, if I find the right buyer."

My heart sank. For a moment I had considered trying to buy the mirror myself.

Either Mr. Colella didn't see my disappointment or he chose to ignore it. "Here," he said, handing me one of his seemingly endless supply of rags. "Polish."

"Probably wouldn't have fit in my room anyway," I muttered as I went to fetch a stepladder so I could reach the top.

Half an hour later I stood back to admire my work but got caught up examining my reflection instead. You could have talked to me all you wanted about inner beauty; I preferred having it outside, where it counted. Not so handsome it scared people off, but definitely good looking. A little too much like my father, though. Sometimes it startled me when I glanced in a mirror and found myself staring at someone who looked just like the guy in the old army photo on our mantelpiece.

Suddenly I noticed a small streak of blood on the mirror. Glancing down at my finger, I saw that the cut had reopened while I was working. I rubbed the rag over the blood, but the mirror wouldn't come clean. I spit on a different finger and tried to rub the blood away. No luck.

I was starting to get angry when the tinkle of the bell above the door announced a customer.

When I came back an hour later, the stain was gone.

Guess Mr. Colella took care of it, I thought, hoping he wouldn't be angry with me for doing a sloppy job. It wouldn't be fair, of course. But like my late father, Mr. Colella tended to yell at me for things that weren't my fault.

I could hardly complain, given my own temper. The thought caused me to scowl at my reflection. Big brown eyes and a try-to-catch-me smile might make it easy to get girls; my sudden bursts of anger sure made it hard to keep them. I rolled my eyes as I remembered yesterday's argument with Gina, which had ended with her slapping me and shouting, "I don't care how cute you are, Jonathan Rawson, I won't be treated this way!"

I put my fingers to my cheek, remembering the slap. Last night I had figured it was time to move on. But Gina was special. Maybe *I* should apologize for a change.

Looking in the mirror to practice my rueful expression, I noticed the beginnings of a pimple beside my nose. I prodded the spot with my fingertips but couldn't feel any bump. Maybe if I was careful it would go away without blossoming into a full-fledged zit.

That seemed to be the case, for when I checked myself in the bathroom mirror at home that night, my skin was smooth and clear.

Whoa! I thought. *Could this be the beginning of the end for zit-osis? What a relief that would be!*

I called Gina to apologize. She was cautious but finally agreed to go out with me on Saturday. I don't know who was more surprised by my apology: Gina, or me.

Humming contentedly, I returned to my desk, where I was building a miniature room for my little sister, Mindy. It was mostly for her birthday. But it was also a way of apologizing to her for all the times I had yelled at her over the last year.

The project had turned out to be a bigger time-sink than I expected. But Mindy had been wanting one of these rooms for years. Our father had promised to make her one several times, but (as usual) he hadn't come through. And now he was gone.

Despite how tricky it was, I found I actually enjoyed the work. And I was really proud of it. I loved seeing each piece come to its final polished perfection. That was one good thing about my job at Mr. Colella's: I had learned a lot about working with wood.

I spent an hour carefully sanding and staining the chair I had finished assembling the night before. When I finally grew so tired I was afraid I would botch the work, I threw Beau, our golden retriever, off the bed and climbed between the sheets.

The next morning my mother overcooked the eggs.

"Sorry, Jon," she said, as she placed the rubbery henfruit in front of me. "I'm not functioning on all cylinders yet. I don't think they're making the coffee as strong as they used to."

"No problem," I said, kissing her on the cheek. "I can manage a tough yolk every now and then."

"Is this *my* kid?" she asked, widening her eyes and

putting a hand on my forehead. "The one who used to have a tantrum if his eggs weren't runny enough to use up all his toast?"

"For Pete's sake, Ma," I said, ducking away from her hand.

School went well, and I had a good time with Gina during art. So I was in a good mood when I got to Mr. Colella's shop.

Mr. Colella, unfortunately, was not. He was standing in front of the Japanese mirror—which was now in the display area—rubbing a rag almost violently over the glass.

A touch of coldness seized my chest when I saw the red streak that marred the surface of the mirror.

"I would have sworn I wiped this off yesterday," said Mr. Colella. He turned and handed me the rag. "Here. You take care of it. And do it right this time!"

He stomped off, banging his leg on an old oak dresser.

I studied the mirror. The red streak was longer than I remembered.

As I reached forward to rub it with the rag, the stain disappeared.

I flinched as if I had been burned. I stared at the mirror, then focused on my own reflection. The spot I had noticed the day before had erupted into an ugly pimple after all.

I put my finger to my face.

The skin was smooth.

I dropped the rag and grabbed both edges of the

mirror, as if I could anchor it into reality. I don't know how long I stood there.

Mr. Colella's voice wrenched me from my trance. "Come on, glamour boy. That mirror's not the only thing in the shop. Get to work!"

I turned away from the mirror. I thought about quickly turning back, to see if it still showed the pimple, and realized I was afraid to do so. I hurried over to Mr. Colella, grateful for an excuse not to have to face myself again.

I avoided the mirror throughout the afternoon.

But if I could avoid it physically, I couldn't keep it out of my thoughts. I tried and discarded a dozen different explanations for the altered reflection: a flaw in the glass, a trick of light, a momentary daydream. Finally I told myself it had simply been an unlikely combination of all of those things, and that I was getting myself wound up over nothing.

My mother met me at the door with a worried look on her face. "Jon, I'm sorry..."

I knew that tone. Something had happened that was going to make me angry, and she was trying to avert the explosion.

"What is it?" I asked tensely.

"Beau..." She waved her hands helplessly. "Well, you should have put it away when you were done last night!"

A sick feeling grabbed me. Pushing past my mother, I ran to my room. I saw the mess with my eyes, but I felt it with my stomach, as solidly as if someone had landed a punch right below my ribs. The miniature room—the five pieces of oak furniture I'd so lovingly crafted, the walls I'd carefully measured and papered— lay in the center of the rug, reduced to nothing more than a pile of wet splinters and dog slobber.

Beau slunk in, drooping his tail and looking guilty.

"You stupid dog!" I shrieked, raising my hand.

"Jonathan!" cried my mother, as Beau whimpered and cowered away.

To my surprise, the storm of anger passed as quickly as it had come. I lowered my hand. Filled with sorrow, I knelt to gather the sodden remains of three months of work. They felt slimy in my hands.

"I'd like to be alone for a little while," I said softly.

Looking at me in astonishment, my mother grabbed Beau by the collar. "I'll call you when supper is ready." But instead of leaving the room, she pushed Beau out, closed the door, and put her arms around me. "It's just that you look so much like your father when you get mad," she whispered.

I laid my head on her shoulder. We both cried.

Monday afternoon Mr. Colella asked if I could stay late to close the shop while he went to an auction. I said I would have to check with my mother. I called, half hoping she would say no. But she okayed the extra hours, and even said she would pick me up after work.

After Mr. Colella left, I found myself glancing un- easily toward the mirror. I shook my head and busied myself with other chores. It was a quiet night; I didn't have a single customer until nearly eight, when Mrs. Hubbard hobbled in. She was one of Mr. Colella's best customers, and it was a relief to see her—though at that point I would have been glad to see *anyone*.

"Hi, Mrs. Hubbard," I said cheerfully. "Can I help you?"

"Just looking tonight, Jonathan," she replied. But a few minutes later she called me over to the mirror.

Reluctantly I crossed to join her.

"This is an interesting piece," she said. "What can you tell me about it?"

"It was made in Japan about three hundred years ago," I said, trying to remember everything Mr. Colella had told me. "We don't know the name of the craftsman, but from the style it appears to have been made in..."

I caught my breath. Couldn't she see it?

"Made in Kyoto?" Mrs. Hubbard prompted, obviously thinking I had forgotten the name of the city.

I hadn't forgotten anything. I was simply too frightened to speak. An inch-wide streak of red had slashed its way across the center of the mirror. That would have been bad enough. But it was the image in the glass that truly terrified me. Two people looked out at me, one a kindly looking elderly woman, the other a strangely altered version of myself. A scattering of open sores stretched from my nose across my right cheek to my hairy, pointed ear.

I glanced at Mrs. Hubbard. She was staring at me expectantly.

I looked back at the mirror.

My reflection smiled at me.

Mrs. Hubbard shook my arm. "Jonathan, are you all right?"

"Don't you see?" I whispered, my voice trembling.

"See what?" she asked, taking a step away from me.

"Nothing. I'm sorry!"

I put my hands over my eyes and pressed them into my face.

She took another step back. "I'll come to see Mr. Colella about the mirror tomorrow." She paused, then looked at me with concern. "Listen to an old woman, Jonathan. I've had my time with mirrors. Don't let them get to you. They're useful, but the truth is, they always lie. Everything is backwards in a mirror. And whatever you see is never more than just a part of you."

I nodded, unable to speak.

She looked at me more closely, then furrowed her brow and said again, "I'll come see Mr. Colella about the mirror tomorrow."

"No, wait!" But it was too late. She had scurried from the shop, leaving me alone with the mirror.

I sidled back to the counter, unwilling to turn my back on the mirror, equally unwilling to look at it. I considered calling my mother and asking her to pick me up early, but couldn't figure out what to give as a reason.

When nine o'clock came I was standing by the door with my hand on the light switch, ready to scoot out as soon as I saw Mom's car.

Tuesday was a good day. Not having to go to the shop, I found myself at peace with the world. Things seemed to be on track with Gina, and the minor annoyances that normally would have made my temper flare seemed unable to affect my good mood.

128

Wednesday afternoon I went to work determined to confront the mirror.

It was gone.

"Mrs. Hubbard bought it yesterday morning," said Mr. Colella. "Said she was going to put it in her front hall. She has a lot of oriental stuff, you know. She and her husband used to live in Japan, before he died. Anyway, I thought you'd be glad it was gone, since it seemed to make you nervous." He paused and looked at me quizzically. "Don't know why. You're a good-looking kid. You shouldn't worry about that kind of thing."

I nodded and set to work, uncertain whether I was relieved or disappointed that the mirror was gone.

Over the next few months I forced myself to forget the mirror. The forgetting was made easier by the fact that my life was taking a turn for the better, as Jonathan the Wild and Temperamental was slowly replaced by Jonathan the Calm and Strong.

"A pleasure to be with" was the way people spoke of me now—the same people who had once avoided me because of my temper. I felt more able to focus on things. My schoolwork improved, and my grades went up. I had more friends.

When I started volunteering at the hospital Gina nicknamed me Saint Jonathan. At first it was a joke, but after a while she began saying it seriously and I sensed that my unswerving calm was actually beginning to worry her.

A month later she broke up with me. Though she wouldn't say why, I had a feeling that I was boring her.

I should have been upset, but I wasn't. For one thing, a half a dozen girls had made it obvious that they would be available if Gina dropped out of the picture. I didn't call any of them, though. Somehow I wasn't that interested.

The horror started in school, oddly enough, where normality seemed to be embedded in the very walls. I was looking in the rest room mirror to adjust my hair when I saw a twisted, evil version of my own face staring back at me.

The image lasted for only a moment. But it left me gasping. Had I really seen it? Or was I having a nervous breakdown?

When I was preparing to go upstairs to bed that night my mother put a hand on my shoulder and said, "I see such a change in you, Jonathan."

I flinched. Had the evil I saw in the mirror started to show on my face? My mother misread my reaction. "Don't be upset. I was trying to tell you how pleased I am. I used to worry you were going to turn out like your father."

I twisted away, started up the stairs.

"Jonathan, I'm sorry! That wasn't fair. Your father had his good qualities. What I meant . . . What I was trying to say . . . was that I was afraid you would have his temper. That it would do to your life what it did to his."

I paused on the stairs but didn't speak.

"Anyway, you seem to be getting a handle on that. I'm pleased. And very proud." She was silent for a moment. "Well, I just wanted to let you know I noticed," she said at last. "Good night, son."

"Good night," I whispered.

Upstairs, I lay staring into the darkness, shaking with terror as I remembered what had happened earlier that day. Finally I climbed out of bed and turned on the light. Whirling around, I saw it again in the mirror over my dresser: a horrifying version of my own face. Though it disappeared almost instantly, I no longer had any doubt that it was real.

Mirrors became my enemy. Though most of the time they were safe, I never knew when I would look into one and see the face that was so much like my own, yet so filled with hate, leering out at me.

It grew worse—uglier and angrier—each time I saw it.

I prayed someone else would see it, so I would know I was not going mad. I also prayed that no one else would see it, for it was far too humiliating.

I stayed away from mirrors as much as possible, even cut my hair short so I wouldn't have to worry about combing it.

"I'm worried about you, Jonathan," said my mother, late that spring. "You seem a little...I don't know, a little thin around the edges. Maybe you're working too hard."

"I'm fine," I said, kissing her on the forehead.

It was a lie, and we both knew it.

"We've got a big house sale," Mr. Colella told me one Friday afternoon. "Former customer passed away and left a huge collection of stuff. No kids. The nieces and nephews live a thousand miles away and all they want is the money. Anyway, I'll need some extra help for the next few days. I want you to come with me."

So the following morning Mr. Colella picked me up in the shop truck and we drove to a large old house. When I saw the mailbox I caught my breath.

Mrs. Hubbard had lived there.

The Japanese mirror stood in the foyer, right where the old woman had told Mr. Colella she was planning to put it all those months ago.

I averted my head as we walked past.

Though I kept myself busy in other parts of the house, the mirror was on my mind all morning. When Mr. Colella left me to continue the inventory while he went to pick up lunch, I found myself drawn irresistibly back to the foyer. I hesitated to enter, but finally a curiosity stronger than terror drove me on. Curiosity... and the hope that perhaps here I could find the answer to the strangeness that had overtaken my life.

I walked slowly toward the mirror. From the angle of my approach I could see the opposite wall reflected in its smooth surface. Everything seemed normal.

I stopped and took a deep breath, then stepped forward and planted myself in front of the mirror.

I screamed.

The wall in the mirror was the same wall that stood behind me. The pictures, the coat rack, and the umbrella stand were all the same. But where I should have seen myself crouched a creature more hideous than anything I had ever imagined.

Blood began to seep down from the top of the mirror. The creature raised its hands and reached forward, reached *toward* me, as if it wanted to snatch me through the glass.

I ran.

In the garden behind the house I threw myself to the ground and sobbed. What made the thing in the mirror so horrible was not horns or scales or anything demonic. What made it horrible was the smoldering rage twisting the features that were all too clearly my own. That, and the understanding that the anger I thought I had escaped for the last six months had been coming here. All my darkness—every vile thought, every angry moment, every instant since October when I had been less than my best—had collected in the mirror, slowly creating a beast that was now nearly strong enough to break out. It was a repository for all that was bad about myself, and what I had seen there was not merely terrifying, it was disgusting.

My mother had said I looked "thin around the edges." Now I understood why: Too much of me had gone into the mirror.

I thought back to the bits of information Mr. Colella had dropped in his usual terse way as we were working. "She died of a heart attack," he had said at one point, for no reason that I could make out. "They found her body in the foyer," he had commented later.

A chill ran over me as I concluded that my other self had scared Mrs. Hubbard to death.

I sat up and wiped my face.

"All right, Saint Jonathan. Now what do you do?"

The answer was simple. The creature had to be destroyed.

But what would that mean to me? The creature was part of me, *was* me, in a way. If I killed it, would I die, too?

Well, saints never hesitated to die for a good cause. Or would this be like committing suicide?

"Jonathan?"

It was Mr. Colella, back with lunch. I took a breath and forced myself to be calm. "Be right there," I called.

I found a hose and washed the tears and dirt from my face.

"What were you doing?" asked Mr. Colella sharply, when I appeared at the door of the kitchen.

I felt an instant of anger at Mr. Colella's tone, then felt the anger disappear. This was a sensation I had experienced often over the last several months. At first I had welcomed it. After a while the feeling had become so familiar that I usually ignored it. Now, though, it horrified me, for I finally understood what it meant. I had just fed my terrible alter ego.

No more free ride, I thought. *I've got to teach myself to be calm for real.*

Doing so took most of my energy for the rest of the day. By the time I went to bed I was exhausted from trying to control my anger. Even so, sleep would not come, and when the alarm I had set to sound at two began to beep, I was still wide awake.

I reached out and snapped it off. Moving slowly, I climbed from my bed and dressed.

Half an hour later I pulled my bike to a halt in front of the Hubbard house. A cool wind whispered around me, making leaves rustle in the darkness. As I traveled up the sidewalk the nearly full moon sent a long shadow stretching ahead of me.

I fumbled in my pocket for the key Mr. Colella had given me earlier that day. Once I had it, I paused. It wasn't too late to turn back.

But the thing waiting inside belonged to me.

So I unlocked the door and stepped inside.

"Hello, *brother*."

I caught my breath. The voice came from the mirror. Had the creature known I was coming? Could it read my mind?

I turned on the light and it appeared immediately, a ravaged parody of my own face staring out from the mirror.

"I've been waiting for you, *Saint* Jonathan," it hissed.

I took a step backward.

The image should have moved back as well, away from me. It didn't. It stayed exactly where it was.

"It's too late for that kind of game, Saint Jonathan. I have a life of my own now. Your mother was right, you know. You *are* getting thinner. Soon there won't be anything left of you. All that goodness will vanish like a puff of smoke in the wind." It laughed. "That's when I'll come back and take over your body. It won't be like dying, not at all like dying. I'm too much a part of you for that, the biggest part of you. Just a few more days —a few more days and we'll be together again."

The eyes looking out at me glowed with an unholy fire.

"Oh, the things we'll do then! We'll start with your

sister, probably. Or maybe your mother. Yes, maybe your mother. That would be nice, don't you think?"

"Stop!" I shouted. I felt the surge of my anger flow into the thing in the mirror and suddenly realized it was goading me, pushing me to give it more strength, more power.

I did the only thing I could think of. Moving as slowly and calmly as I could manage, I turned to the umbrella stand behind me. I picked it up. Then I threw it into the mirror.

The glass shattered. The pieces crashed and tinkled to the floor.

My sense of triumph lasted only a second. With a sudden hiss a flare of blue light crackled around the black lacquer frame.

A moment later my other self came crawling over the edge.

"How kind of you to set me free. Earlier than I expected, but not unwelcome. No, not unwelcome at all."

It lunged at me. I screamed and jumped back as my own face, burning with hatred, riddled with oozing sores, surged up at me. I dodged to the right, racing around the creature. It clutched at me. I jumped forward, tripped over the black lacquer frame—and fell into the reverse world of the mirror.

The creature followed close behind me. I could hear it scrabbling on the floor, panting, not from exertion, but from a lust to possess me.

"I don't want you!" I cried as I ran through the mirror version of Mrs. Hubbard's house. "I don't want you. You're not part of me anymore!"

"I've always been part of you," laughed the creature. "And now *you* will be part of *me* ... Saint Jonathan."

The last words were spit out with such contempt that I felt my fear double. If this thing that hated me so much were to catch me, what would it do to me? *What would it do to those I loved?*

I stumbled around a corner, regained my balance, saw a door and a stairwell. I took the stairs rather than the door, because to lead this thing out of the house and into the world—even the mirror world—was too awful.

I was halfway up the stairs when I heard my mother's voice call, "Jonathan! Jonathan, wait for me!"

I turned back. But the voice had come from the creature. It was standing at the base of the stairs, leering up at me. A string of drool dangled from its pendulous lower lip.

I turned to run, and gasped. Above me, floating at the top of the stairs, was Mrs. Hubbard. A pale glow surrounded her translucent figure.

"I'm sorry, Mrs. Hubbard!" I cried. "I didn't know what was happening. I didn't mean for you to die!"

"Don't be foolish!" she snapped. "Listen to me, Jonathan. Remember what I told you. Mirrors always lie. Everything is backwards here. Now you have to want him more than he wants you."

"What do you mean?"

But her image vanished, shimmering out of sight like a reflection in a pond when the water is disturbed.

A snarl from behind sent me bolting the rest of the way up the stairs.

You have to want him more than he wants you.

137

I stumbled along a hallway.

"Jonathan, you're mine. Stop running."

Stop running. That wouldn't be good enough. I had to stop being afraid. The creature was feeding on my fear, growing stronger every moment.

You have to want him more than he wants you.

I stopped. Heart pounding, I turned to face the creature.

It paused, looking wary.

Summoning every ounce of courage I possessed, I spread my arms and whispered, "Come back."

The creature's eyes widened. It hissed.

I took a step toward it.

It backed away, still hissing.

I took another step. It turned and ran. I raced after it, caught it with a flying tackle at the head of the stairs.

"No!" it screamed, struggling to escape my grasp. "Get back!"

I was too sure to let go now. I clutched it to me, for it was my own. Screaming, it clawed its way forward until it managed to pull both itself and me over the edge of the stairs.

We tumbled down, rolling over and over, thumping and bouncing. It hurt like hell, but I didn't let go. When we hit the bottom, I was on top. Wrapping my arms around the creature, I pulled it to me and whispered, "You're mine. You're mine, and I claim you."

I could feel it wavering, growing thinner in my arms. But it was still struggling, still real and solid.

Stronger now, I pinned it to the floor. I stared at that fierce and horrid face—my own face, twisted and ravaged by all my anger. Pushing past my disgust, my revulsion, I pressed my cheek to the creature's.

"You're mine," I whispered in its ear. "Welcome home."

Then I held it as close to my heart as I could, and howled in sorrow and triumph as my lost anger seared its way back into my soul.

The beast vanished from beneath me.

I collapsed to the floor, where I lay for a long time, weeping but whole, Saint Jonathan no longer.

"Not bad kid," said a deep, dear voice, once so familiar, now nearly forgotten. "Not bad at all."

I looked up and saw my father smiling down at me, translucent and shimmering as Mrs. Hubbard had been.

I reached out toward him, but he shook his head sadly and began to fade from sight. "Can't do it, kid. I'm breaking the rules as it is. But I wanted to let you know you did good."

"Don't go! I need you!"

"I know. You always needed me. And I was never there."

He shimmered back into view and stepped closer. Fearful, I started to draw back but forced myself to stay.

My father lifted his hand. I whimpered at the sight. How often when I was five, six, seven had I seen that hand rise like this to strike me? But there was no anger now, only deep, enduring sorrow as the memory of flesh came down to brush against my cheek.

I swiped at a tear, trying to hide it, too aware of how my tears had always stirred my father's wrath.

"I always loved you, Jonathan," he whispered, his voice cracking. "I was just too dumb to say it."

He put his arms around me, embracing me as I had embraced the creature, and though no touch could be felt it was as real as salt and deep as love itself.

Then, before I could say a word, he was gone.

After a time I got to my feet.

Moving slowly, I walked toward the frame. I glanced back only once. There was nothing behind me.

Turning, I stepped through the black lacquer frame, back to where my own sweet, harsh world lay waiting.

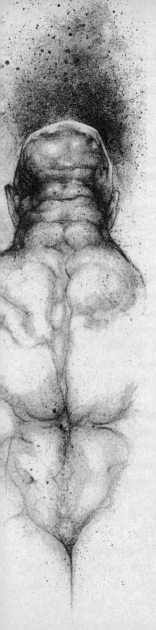

ALAN SMALE

THE SMOOTH MAN

We had arranged to meet at seven at the end of Faith's street, in the estate that I thought of as a purpose-built slum, all cinder blocks and prefabricated panels. Faith didn't come out with us anymore but we hung around there anyway, hoping to embarrass her with her new boyfriend.

Steve had arrived first. "All right?" he said, our standard greeting.

"All right, our Steve," I said. My parents were originally from Surrey, but I turned on the Leeds accent when I walked out of the house. "Where's Kenny, then?"

He shrugged and sniffed.

Steve had the reddest hair and the biggest ears I'd ever seen. He was short and wiry, the kind of kid whose sleeves are always four inches too long for his arms. He bunched his cuffs into his fists so you couldn't see his hands. Even when he was clean, he looked dirty.

His dark little eyes locked on target. "Belfield alert."

I followed his gaze. "Great," I said. "Why's Kenny bringing *him* along?"

Phil Belfield was definitely no friend of mine. At our last meeting he'd kicked my shins with his football boots in the changing rooms at school. He did stuff like this all the time—in the last two weeks he'd also pushed me into a wall, tripped me on the stairs, and held a burning match to my arm. Young for my school year, and no good at sports, I was considered fair game by several of the harder jock types.

Most of my classmates, I knew, would live and die in Yorkshire. But not me. I planned to work hard, get the grades, and get out. London, America—anywhere would do. Success is the best revenge.

"Hey," said Kenny. "Look what I found down at the shops."

I wasn't going to let this slide. "If you'd found a dog poop, would you have brought that, too?"

Belfield sneered cheerfully. "Hard man, aren't you?"

Kenny flashed me the look that meant my mouth was getting me into trouble. He thought he was smart, chumming up to Belfield, but it would all be forgotten the next time Belfield needed an easy laugh at our expense at school. "So are we off, then?" I said. We started walking.

If I'd thought Belfield would just melt away, I was wrong. "My old man brought a head home the other night," he said. "A *human* head." He drew a line across his throat with his finger and stuck his tongue out.

"Right," said Steve.

"He *did*," said Belfield. "He's an ambulance driver. This woman killed herself up on the railway line. My dad had to go and clean it up. Anyway, he stopped in at our house on the way back. In he comes with this head tucked underneath his arm, doing Mary, Queen of Scots. My mother went crackers."

So that was where Belfield got his sense of humor.

"What a spin," said Steve. He would know. He could spin a good yarn himself when he felt like it.

"Want to bet?" Belfield's hand was out.

"Has he still got it, then?"

" 'Course not. He took it to the hospital."

"Spin, spin, spin," said Steve. "Surprised you're not dizzy."

I sighed. Belfield's gangling presence had locked us into an endless loop of macho banter.

Even so, he seemed bored. "Anyway, what do you all *do*? Just walk around like this all the time?"

Well, what *did* we do? It was 1974; we were too young to go into discos but not old enough for it to bother us much. We went around to each others' houses and listened to records. We went to Carl's and played bridge, and tried not to get caught signaling to each other. We messed with a Ouija board from time to time; the dead never cooperated, although sometimes we got a message from Kenny.

Hanging around on street corners was mostly what we *did* do.

"We do gardens," said Kenny suddenly.

Uh-oh.

"What?" said Belfield. "For money? Sounds awful."

"Not *gardening*," I said. "He means we sneak through people's gardens, exploring. If you start at my house there's about a hundred gardens in a row. An acre or more each. Lots of trees and lawns and stuff."

"Ours is about the size of a Ping-Pong table," said Belfield, but his interest was pricked. "D'you find anything worth nicking? I bet you see girls undressing in their bedroom windows all the time."

"We don't steal," said Steve, in disgust.

"We don't spy, either," I added.

"You two should get married," said Belfield. "So, are we going to do this or d'you just get your cheapies talking about it?" *Cheapies* were cheap thrills, unworthy pleasures that real men like Belfield didn't stoop to.

When we did gardens, it was in daylight and was an exercise in covert action and exploring the unknown. Theft and property damage weren't any part of it. And besides, we'd stopped doing it months ago. After a few times it just started to feel . . . wrong. Like I was reaching toward something that wasn't meant to be touched.

"We haven't done it for a while," I said.

"I'm surprised *you* do it at all," said Belfield. "I thought nice boys didn't trespass."

"It was my idea in the first place," I said, stung. "I invented it."

There was a pause. *"Well?"* said Belfield.

Kenny and Steve were waiting for me to say no, so they wouldn't have to do it but would have somebody else to blame. I didn't want to do it, either, not at all. But I was in a corner now, with no way out. Nobody was going to call me chicken about *doing gardens,* of all things. I knew gardens.

If anything, we were even less likely to get caught at night.

Maybe Belfield would fall in someone's ornamental pond.

I adopted the proper bored expression. "Let's go."

When Belfield jumped over the fence from the common land into my garden, I felt violated.

This was my private territory, the secret domain of a childhood spent largely alone watching the bugs on the roses near the house, the termites in the old stump, and the frogs and newts in the murky depths of the pond. If I lay very still in the bushes up at the top of the garden, screened from the house by poplars and rhododendrons, I sometimes glimpsed a rusty tail as a fox skittered through the long grass.

An ancient sycamore maple grew just to the right of where we were standing. It was the first really tall tree I had ever climbed when I was a little kid, and from its dizzy heights I'd seen the roof of our house poking up above the foliage, and the street winding gently like a river to the north, lined by our neighbors' gardens, each a separate world. Lawns and broadleaf oaks heavy with ivy, stands of silver birch that trembled in the slightest breeze, drystone walls and hedges, and on the horizon the purple-gray beginnings of the Yorkshire Dales.

Then I'd felt so *strong*. Such a spunky kid. Nothing had scared me. Now, thanks to people like Belfield, I knew I was weak.

Back in the here and now, the sun had set, but there was enough twilight for Belfield to see the scrubgrass area that used to be our third lawn. An oak a hundred feet tall crowned a low rise nearby.

"All this belongs to one house?" said Belfield.

I marched them across my garden to the stone wall that separated us from Muriel's. This far up, her house and mine were invisible behind the trees. I hopped the wall.

Their top lawn was in better shape than ours. Before her son, Chris, left home, they used to play tennis on it.

As we went, the three of us who were old pros stepped over each fallen twig, but Belfield hit them all, *snap-snap-snap*. At least I always knew where he was.

The snapping stopped, and I looked around. He was throwing a stone at a squirrel. It was a long shot, but he nearly hit it.

"Cut it out," I said.

"Yes, sir. Sorry, sir."

Another drystone wall. As Belfield marched over it, hands back in his pockets, he knocked a couple of rocks onto the grass. I stopped to rebuild the wall. He gave me a strange look, but I didn't say anything.

I knew next-door-but-one had a golden retriever, so we went across that one *fast*, and I kept up the pace through the next two. If anybody was going to catch us, I wanted them to be strangers. A crescent moon emerged from the darkening sky to light the way, but Belfield still stumbled every third step.

"Enough of the nature walk," said Belfield. "I thought we were going to see people's *houses*."

The other two deferred to me. Gardens were "my game." I waited a couple of seconds to make sure Belfield got the message, then said, "Not yet," and led us on.

As we went up Hillcrest Rise, we went up the social scale, and tall privet hedges rather than drystone walls formed the boundaries between gardens. Hedges have their own logic, and it's easier to get through them where they're punctuated by trees. I was beyond known territory now, often having to hunt for a good route. We all got scratched a few times. Belfield tripped a lot but failed to land in a pond.

Breathing the woody smells of pine, heather, and grass, and seeking out new paths, I almost enjoyed the novelty of leading a group that contained Phil Belfield.

"How about that way?"

He was turned around. The houses had to be dead left of where we were.

The troops were getting restless, and I was out of excuses. At least it was properly dark now. Silently, I led the way down the garden till a house emerged from the shrubbery. Three windows showed lights, two eyes and a nose.

"Is *your* house that big?" said Belfield.

"Quiet," I said. "Sound travels at night. Yes, it's about that size."

"You git. What does your dad do?"

"He's a manager for the TV company."

A woman was standing in her kitchen facing the open window, looking down at her hands and nodding her head in time to a melody we could not hear. As we watched, she lifted a wet plate from the sink and put it in a drying rack to her left. From where she stood we'd be invisible behind her own image, reflected in the glass.

"Let's give her a fright," said Belfield. "Let's go closer till she sees us. She'll jump a mile."

"Let's not," said Steve.

"Scared?"

"Is that how you get your cheapies?" I said. "Saying boo to little old ladies? You're pretty hard."

Belfield loomed. "You want to fight about it?"

A high yipping made us jump. "Foxes," I said. "Want to track them?"

"Why?" said Belfield.

We went on.

The next garden was beautiful. The rockeries were landscaped, flowers in bloom, the lawns manicured and neatly edged. We passed the mother of greenhouses as we came in, and out of the corner of my eye I saw Belfield staring. I was checking the house. A dim light showed from behind the bedroom curtain, maybe another on the stairs. They were probably out, with the lights left on to deter burglars.

Belfield was getting antsy. "There's too much money around here. It makes me sick. You dirtbags all own

148

your own *forest*. I bet that greenhouse cost more than our *street*."

"Shut up. Somebody'll hear."

"Yeah," said Belfield. "They'll hear, all right."

And he picked up a great big stone and chucked it straight into the greenhouse.

It was a good shot. Somehow he took out about four panes of glass in one go, and it sounded like one of those TV shows where the bomb goes off inside the abandoned factory and all the windows blow out. It went on for about a week. Worse, a strut gave out after the first panes went, and the release of tension broke a whole bunch more glass.

Lights went on in that house, and in both neighbors' houses. Steve and Kenny were already running. Belfield just rocked on his heels, hands in pockets, smiling strangely. "That'll teach them," he said. "Then when they fix it, I'll come back and smash the hell out of it again."

Somewhere a dog was barking. Kenny disappeared into the bushes on Steve's tail, floodlights were coming on, and there I was, standing in the middle of enemy territory, trying to get Belfield to move.

"Come *on*," I said, "you stupid git—"

All in one movement, he turned and hit me in the face. Big blobs of light exploded behind my eyes and the crashing started again, this time in my head. As I fell down he jumped over me and high-tailed it after the others.

Doors slamming. Adult male voices, two.

I stood up, not sure where I was, and lights splashed my chest.

I *ran*.

I passed a big bush, iron-edged in the harsh lighting, and swerved to get behind it. The first root or ornamental pond would take me out of the game—I couldn't recognize a likely tree or hiding place with the stars still in my eyes. Best to go on, get out of the garden.

I hit the hedge running. It snagged my clothes and pulled me backward, but I made it through without losing too much speed.

Somebody was close behind me. I didn't look back.

Big trees in the next garden. Every time I went by one I changed direction.

The footfalls behind me faded away. Adults rarely trespass on their neighbors' turf, even in hot pursuit. I glanced over my shoulder and saw nobody. I jogged on a bit farther for good measure, then sagged behind a tree, opening my mouth wide so I could pant without gasping.

This had to be a big garden, much bigger than the others. I'd run a long way without going over a wall or through another hedge. I walked quietly down toward the house, to get my bearings.

A thousand paces and no house. Just trees and heavy undergrowth.

I pictured it in my mind, from above. Hillcrest Rise and Briar Lane made two sides of a long, thin triangle with wavy sides, and we'd been heading toward the school at the apex. I couldn't have walked that far without seeing a house. This was impossible.

I crouched and felt a mulch of leaves and tiny twigs.

Old-forest covering, the type that takes centuries to make, not domestic landscaping gone wild.

Something was nagging at me, some nasty old memory that nibbled at the edge of my mind. But when I moved my head to get a glimpse of it, the memory moved, too. I shivered.

"Steve?" I said. The forest swallowed up the sound. "Kenny?"

I tried again in a hundred yards, and Belfield answered me.

He was standing looking up at the trees. I approached warily. Wherever we were, this was a good opportunity for him to finish what he'd started.

"If you try to tell me *this* all belongs to one house, I'm going to push your face in," he said. He was in shadow, but the tone of his voice told me it was meant to be banter.

"Funny," I said. "I wasn't about to tell you that."

"What woods are these?"

"I don't know. They shouldn't be here."

I waited for him to scoff, but he just nodded.

Then he spun around so dramatically that I ducked. "Somebody's watching us."

My night sight was back to normal, but I could barely see Belfield, let alone a mystery intruder. "This isn't a council estate. There are a million birds and animals here. Of course we're being watched."

He stared off into the gloom. "You never give it up, do you? So superior all the time. And you wonder why everybody hates you."

I thought about that for the next few moments while Belfield hunted around for hidden surveillance units.

"Did you feel it when we first came in here?" he said.

"What?"

"Like some kind of a jolt, going through the hedge?"

"No," I said.

"It was like being hit by a bus," he said. "So you don't know everything, then. Amazing. Well, come on."

I wanted to ask him where he thought he was going, but I didn't want to be superior, so I just tagged along behind.

By day I knew the trees. I could recognize them by their leaves, their bark, their fruit, their shapes. By night they merged together into a huge anonymous mass. Tendrils and brambles snatched at my legs. Twigs reached out to touch my nose and cheeks. A light breeze stirred the leaves around me and nudged at the hairs on the back of my neck.

Belfield stopped dead and pointed. I caught a glimpse of yellow, then it was gone.

"I hate the outdoors," he muttered.

We stumbled on. I was getting spooked, so I reached out to the trees as I passed, and they became friends again: the furrowed bark of an oak, the smooth sheen of a beech. But I also touched the serrated leaves of elms, the oval supporting leaves of mountain ash, even larches and spruce, trees I'd never seen in the area. Worse, for every three trees I recognized, there was one that was unknown to me.

And that elusive memory needled me again. *Something about the quiet whisper of the wind, or the smell of the forest mold...*

152

I grabbed Belfield's arm.

"Don't touch me," he said. "What is it?"

It was my turn to point.

A figure stood on a branch at head height. Man-shaped, but just twelve inches tall. I could see the glint of yellow in its eyes, and the shadows of shaggy hair and torn clothes. It leaned on a spear the size of a letter opener.

The imp said something. It sounded like Gaelic, spoken with a Yorkshire accent. Then Belfield's stone hit it in the chest, and it squawked and tumbled backward into the brush.

I stared at him aghast. "What did you do that for?"

"I don't believe in fairies. Come on."

Then, as we approached a clearing in the wood, a circle open to the gray skies, we found Steve. He was swinging back and forth like a pendulum, suspended upside down by his ankles at the end of a long rope. At the bottom of each wide arc his red hair grazed the forest floor.

We ran and grabbed the rope as it went by, to bring him to a stop. I was ready for him to be a corpse, but what I'd taken for the rictus of death was just Steve screwing up his face, fighting dizziness and fear.

"All right," hissed Belfield. "What's going on?"

Steve gulped. "Get me down. I feel awful."

I ran my hands over the knots. "It might take awhile. Steve, who did this to you?"

Steve spit on the ground. "Smooth Man," he said. "Smooth Man. And watch out for the small ones. They got knives."

The Smooth Man. "Yes," I said. "Yes, that's it. I remember now."

I was seven years old, in the garden. Waiting for the foxes, I drifted off to sleep in a scooped-out hollow beneath the skeleton of a long-fallen tree. I dreamed that a man came out of one of the living trees, a big fat pulpy man, and leaned over me as I slept. A dozen snakes slithered at his feet, impatient to creep into my clothing and share my warmth. The man held them back, but from caution, not kindness. He passed a hand over my closed eyes, and I awoke. I jumped up and slapped my clothes in panic, but the hissing of the snakes had become the whisper of the late breeze in the trees, and I was quite alone.

Just an old dream? Or more than a dream?

Now I knew why we were here, wherever *here* was. We hadn't come by accident. It was my fault. My link to this place had been forged all those years ago, when I was seven and strong. My connection to the wild places of the garden had let me reach beyond what was local and comfortable and known. In my drowsiness I had drifted toward this world and touched something that was truly wild. Something that knew me and responded to me and took a piece of my strength. Something that hadn't forgotten me, and had reached back in its turn to nudge at my senses when I'd trespassed into the strange gardens of my neighbors.

Something that had pulled us all here.

"For heaven's *sake*," said Belfield. "Are you going to untie him or *what?*"

He was right, for once. I looked at the ground for a sharp stone—and jumped out of my skin. Six feet away, a dozen imps stared at me balefully. More crowded up behind me.

And...

At first I took it for an afterimage of the sky, or a pale moonbeam shining on a bush, but then it moved and became flesh.

And *flesh* was the word. I was staring at a human figure a foot taller than me and two feet broader. A pudgy face set on top of a full frame, with skin that glowed with a cold inner light. His jowls were loose around his neck, and he was girdled with a pallid tire of blubber. He was naked, but there was nothing comical about him. Icy sweat trickled down my neck.

Yep, that was him.

"Belfield," I said.

"I see him. Big git. I'll sort *him* out."

"Be careful," I said. "I've seen him before. I had a dream when I was younger."

"Get a grip," said Belfield. "This is *real*."

The Smooth Man flowed toward us. Fat men are sometimes ungainly, but this one almost glided through the undergrowth, untouched by the twigs and thorns that tripped mere mortals. I could see every bland feature of his face now, purposeful but with no personality. His hands hung limp and empty by his sides, but he had the shoulders of a sumo. I took two steps backward.

Hot pain sliced through my calf. I kicked out and an imp spun away into the darkness, but I could feel blood soaking my left jeans leg. The other imps shuffled to close the gap in their ranks.

Belfield charged. He jumped over the first line of imps easily enough, but when he swerved and tried to jump again he went down, tripped by something I couldn't see. He had covered less than half the distance to the Smooth Man.

He started screaming.

I leaped for the rope, scrambled up over Steve's body and away from the ground; climbed, trying not to think about what might happen next, praying there were no imps above me in the tree. With Steve weighing down the end of the rope I couldn't use my feet properly, and my biceps popped like bowstrings.

I felt a branch above my head and batted at it, expecting any second to feel the sting of a blade across the tendons of my wrist. When it didn't come I hauled myself up, got a leg over the branch, and lay flat, sucking air into my lungs. Thirty feet below, the Smooth Man watched me impassively, and the imps fussed and boiled on the ground like snakes in a pit.

A small wicker cage had appeared in the center of the clearing. I watched as ten of the little beasts dragged Belfield's prone body into it and tied the door closed.

The hissing grew louder. Imps were climbing the tree.

I crawled to the trunk and used it to drag myself to my feet. My knees were trembling so hard that I had to push them into the bark to keep my legs straight. Blood still poured out of my ankle.

I climbed. It wasn't easy, but I would rather have fallen and broken my neck than waited for those evil little creatures to catch me. I had no knife, no plan, no nothing. I was just heading for altitude.

Kenny's voice, shouting and swearing. I looked down just in time to see him go into the cage and hear

Belfield telling him to watch where he was putting his feet.

Sixty feet up, I figured I was high enough. The branches were close enough together that I could wedge myself firmly in place. I looked down. Below me the trunk of the tree rippled as the imps climbed after me. My heart banged in my chest like a hammer.

I pulled off my left shoe and tied the laces into a noose around my wrist. The sock was slippery with blood, and when I ripped it off the pain made me scream and pound my fist into the tree trunk. What I needed was a stone to put in the sock; instead, I dropped my watch, keys, and money into it and thwacked it against a branch a few times. I heard glass tinkle, but the sock seemed heavy enough.

Then I waited for the little swine to slither into range.

I swung the shoe at the end of its laces and scored a cold shot to the head of the first imp. It peeled off the tree and disappeared into the murk below. I heard it bouncing off branches, hissing like a burst pipe. I tried my other weapon on the second one but it clung to the sock, and I had to slam it into the bark five or six times before it cracked open and tumbled away.

A spear jabbed into my good leg and I kicked out, almost tumbling out of my lair. I heard a crunch and smelled blood and metal. After that it all merged into a blur as I flailed and shouted and screamed and pounded, and my assailants traded their lives for a cut here, a slash there.

When I came back to myself, I was drenched with sweat and blood, not all of it mine.

I drummed my feet on a tree branch, punched the sky, heard myself giggling. "Hey, Belfield, you turkey!" I shouted. "Now I know what it's like to beat up the little guys!"

Two faces peered up at me from the cage. Nobody answered me. I replayed the raw, flaky sound of my voice in my head and tried to shut up. I was being too loud again.

At the foot of the tree, a pale figure paced. I could hear the strange Gaelic being spoken, and a lot of hissing. Some kind of argument was going on. I closed my eyes, and my mind went on vacation for a few seconds.

When I raised my head, Steve was crammed into the cage with the others and my tree was quivering as the Smooth Man clambered onto the lower branches. His broad shoulders bulged. He did not look up or down as he climbed.

The fear had washed out of me by now. I felt cold. I wondered what death would be like.

I started to climb again. Maybe if I went high enough, the branches would be too slender to bear his weight and he wouldn't be able to follow.

But, no, it wouldn't matter. With those arms, he'd just shake me off the tree like a plum.

The Smooth Man pulled himself higher, moving slowly and carefully. Every time he stepped onto a branch the whole tree shook. I had plenty of time to watch, because the higher he came, the slower he got.

In the fragile top growth, with my feet braced against branches slimmer than my wrist, I stopped. Six feet above me the last leaves brushed the sky. Across the valley I saw no streetlights, no houses. The lay of the land was familiar, but woods and meadows stretched away to the horizon.

A moon a few days past full shone from the wrong part of the sky. I untied the shoe from my wrist.

When the Smooth Man reached the branch where I'd fought my battle, he lifted his bald head and looked at me. I saw sunken eyes in a puffy face, and a mouth straight as a line. But there was something more behind the eyes, something that hadn't been there on the ground.

A subtle vibration in the tree gave me the clue.

The Smooth Man was terrified.

Beneath him the jabbering redoubled like a curse. He looked down at the ground so far below, and at the creatures that drove him; and up, at the stranger who'd invaded his land.

I felt almost sorry for him, just for a second.

"Go down," I said. "Leave me alone."

He looked at me blankly.

"I didn't mean to come here," I said. "It wasn't my fault. Just let me go, or . . ." What?

His eyes burned into mine. I couldn't read them.

Did he shrug? Was that a grimace of resignation? "Go down," I repeated.

Then he reached out a trembling hand to the next branch, and I hurled the shoe into his face.

His head jerked as the heel struck him on the nose. He shifted his weight to avoid the next missile, and his foot slipped on a broad patch of my blood. Suddenly his arms were taking all his weight, and there was a harsh crack as the living timber sheared.

Stupidly, crazily, I reached out to save him. Stupid

because he was fifteen feet out of my reach, crazy because he outweighed me four to one. I slid dangerously close to disaster before I caught myself.

He was gone. In slow motion the Smooth Man bounced off the first branch, smashed through the next, and spun in a broad arc to the ground. There was a dull thud, and then silence. Leaves fluttered through the air like moths as the light within him dimmed and went out.

And the imps fell on his body in fury, hissing their hatred into the night. I understood at last. He had lost face with them, and their bleating and barking as he climbed had been aimed at him, not me. He had been their leader until he'd shown weakness, and then it was all over. For the first time I saw how that worked, and I realized that even as I had known the Smooth Man, he had known me, too.

The imps seethed and hissed on the ground below. Well, if they had been his fears, they were mine now.

I clambered down the tree.

Six or seven solid ranks of imps blocked my way to the cage where my friends were trapped. Blood covered their spears. I walked straight into their midst and my vision blurred. Were they snakes after all? Demons? I wasn't sure. But they parted to let me go by.

For a moment I was seven years old again. Strong.

I unlaced the door of the wicker basket. "You owe me one, Belfield. Remember this."

"Don't let it go to your head. You were lucky."

"That's me from now on," I said. "Mr. Lucky. Now, let's get out of here. Don't run. Don't show fear."

We walked, and the wet sounds of the imps' butchery faded. We walked in a straight line, and when we came to a dark drystone wall we climbed it and went on without looking back.

We never told anybody, of course. They would have thought it was a colossal spin. We never did gardens again. We even threw the Ouija board away.

Belfield didn't bully me anymore. He didn't exactly stand up for me, either, but when other boys picked on me he would distract them if he could do it without being too obvious.

I tried standing up for myself, showing no fear. Sometimes it helped, sometimes I just got it worse; there are no easy answers. But it seemed to me that I blunted the edge of their contempt. The rest of my school life sailed by like a dream.

Steve, always torn between becoming a tramp or an accountant, chose the latter. Before long he bought himself a rather large house with a very small garden. I lost touch with Kenny after he enrolled at the local college and moved into town.

Belfield, believe it or not, joined the police.

And me? I stuck to the plan. As soon as I turned eighteen I got the hell out of Yorkshire. And I never went back.

DEBRA DOYLE AND
JAMES D. MACDONALD

UP THE AIRY MOUNTAIN

As soon as I put down the
phone on Saturday morning I
knew that Val was planning to
get herself killed.

All she'd said was, "I found
a place that didn't smell right,
so I thought I'd go check it out
in the daytime."

I said, "Wait for me," and
that was it.

Thing is, Val thinks she's
immortal. I know she isn't. So
I grabbed my backpack from
behind my bedroom door and

went out to the pickup. I had to brush a layer of fresh snow off the Beast's windshield before I could see well enough to drive. I hadn't gone anywhere off the farm since getting back from school on Friday afternoon before it started snowing, even though there'd been a dance later that same night and I sort of have a steady girlfriend.

But the sort-of-girlfriend is Val, and Val...well, Val is a werewolf. It means she can't eat pizza because of the garlic; she's always hungry because all that supernatural healing ability, strength, and speed have to get their energy from somewhere; and she doesn't approve of the Lone Ranger because of those silver bullets. I like her anyway. Want to make something out of it? What it all boils down to is, the reason I wasn't at the dance was because Val wasn't at the dance, and Val wasn't at the dance because Friday night was the full moon, and she was off running through the hills and howling.

This time she'd found something out there that she didn't like. I was just glad that she'd bothered to give me a call before heading back for a second look.

I drove into town and met her at her house. She came out looking great, like she always does, dressed for the weather in a long blue coat, high boots, and a red knit cap and mittens. Too classy for a guy with farm dirt on his boots, so I felt lucky.

"Where to?" I asked as she slid into the pickup.

She kicked the ammo box full of wrenches and old spark plugs out of the way of her feet and fastened her seat belt before she answered. "Down to the school."

That wasn't what I'd expected, but it was her call.

I said, "Okay," put the Beast in gear, and off we went.

When we got there, the parking lot was mostly empty. I parked near the fence beside the baseball field. The same snowfall that had blanked out the Beast's windshield had covered the field, and the January sunlight came off it bright enough to make me squint.

I got out and grabbed my backpack. I swung it on and cinched the straps tight. Val made a face—she could smell what was inside the pack, no question, but she didn't say anything. I've kept that pack stocked and ready ever since I found out the hard way that werewolves aren't the only things out there.

"You came here last night?" I asked her.

She blushed a little; I don't know why. "Just running around. Following scents, the way I do. The dance was about over when I came by. People were leaving—most of them were already gone. And I saw a couple leaving together, a guy and a girl. The guy I didn't know. The girl was Candi."

I had to think for a moment before I could place the name. "Candi Ellison? From your homeroom?"

"That's the one." Val looked a bit shamefaced for a moment. "I don't know her all that well...She lives over on the other side of town, and I think her family is kind of strict. I'm surprised they finally let her come to a dance."

"So she left with a guy." I still wasn't certain what Val was driving at. "Then what? Did they go out necking or something?"

"That's what I want to find out." It was cold in the parking lot, and Val's breath was curling like steam around her face. "We have to follow my tracks from last night." She nodded across at the baseball field, with the woods backing it. "That way."

She didn't waste any more time in talking. Instead she made a run at the chain-link fence and jumped it, grabbing the bar at the top and swinging herself over. All that touched the fence were her hands, and that fence is eight feet high.

Werewolves are stronger than the rest of us. A lot stronger. I walked down the fence a few yards and went in at the gate.

Val was waiting for me at the edge of the baseball field, looking out toward the bleachers on the far side. The snow was fresh, and mostly unmarked. Any tracks would show up nice and clear. In fact, I spotted them first.

I pointed at the pawprints in the snow. "You?" I asked. Dumb question, really—it was either her or the biggest dog I'd ever seen.

"Yip yip," she said. "It sure wasn't Lassie in duck-boots."

That was when I realized that she was really scared. Things that would make anyone else start screaming, make Val come up with dumb wisecracks. I ran through my own mental list of things bad enough to frighten a werewolf, and started getting nervous myself.

We started walking parallel to the wolf prints. "There," Val said after we'd gone a little way, and pointed.

I looked, and saw more tracks converging with the wolf prints: boots, this time, two sets of them, side by side. The strides matched, even though one set of prints was a lot smaller than the other.

"The guy was taller than Candi?" I asked.

She had to think about the answer for a moment. I don't know what the world feels like to a wolf—Val doesn't talk about it much—but I get the impression sometimes that how things look isn't all that important to her during the full moon.

"Yes," she said after a bit. "Taller. He smelled funny, though. So I followed them."

"What kind of funny?"

She took awhile longer to answer the question this time. Hunting for the right word, I guess.

"Would it help if I told you, Like nothing I've ever smelled before?"

"Not particularly," I said, but I was fibbing a little. I didn't know whether to relax or not. Her answer did rule out a couple of possibilities. Val says vampires smell like dead things and werewolves have the wolf smell on them no matter what form they're in, but just because we weren't dealing with either one of those didn't mean that we were safe. There's more weird stuff loose in the world than you think.

We followed the boot tracks, and the wolf tracks that shadowed them at a little distance, on across the snowy field and into the woods. The state highway runs along the other side of the property, so I figured we couldn't get too lost. There's thirteen acres out back of the school still wooded over—every couple of years somebody tries to buy up the land and develop it, but the developers always wind up in some kind of legal tangle and the plan gets dropped.

Pretty soon we couldn't see any buildings, just trees all around. The noises of cars and people faded away,

166

and I could hear Val's breathing, fast and nervous and almost as loud as my own. I kept my eyes on the boot tracks as they went on deeper into the trees. Then Val stopped.

"That's where it began," she said. "See?"

I sure did. Right about where we were standing, the guy's tracks changed. They weren't boot prints any longer; the marks in the snow'd been left by something smaller, rounder, and split up the middle. Cloven hooves.

"Yeah," I said. I was thinking about all the things that have goat hooves like that. Some of them make werewolves and vampires look like kid stuff. "Did you happen to catch what he turned into?" I thought about the stuff in my backpack while I waited for her answer. Depending on what she said next, I might or might not have some things in there that could come in useful.

She shook her head. "He didn't change size any, and he smelled the same as before. That's all I noticed." She gave me a quick grin with a lot of teeth in it—another hint that she wasn't as calm as she pretended. "Don't worry. It just keeps on getting better."

We followed the trail a little farther—the boots and the wolf tracks and the cloven hooves—until we came to a patch of open ground, a kind of natural clearing. That's where the hoofprints stopped, and Candi's boots along with them. And when I say *stopped,* I don't mean that they slowed down or changed direction or anything like that. I mean disappeared—vanished—do not pass GO and do not collect two hundred dollars. Poof.

"Well," I said. I tried to sound calmer than I felt. "What happened here?"

Val shook her head. "I don't know. It was dark, and I wasn't *that* close. But the smells...they got weirder than I could handle. All I could think of was getting out of here as fast as I could."

"I get the picture." More than she thought I did, probably. If something had frightened her enough to make her run away, no wonder she'd insisted on coming straight back as soon as the moon was down and the sun was up. Val can't handle being scared. It makes her reckless.

Me, I figure being scared is nature's way of saying, *You'll be* SOOORRY. But, okay, I was getting curious. Right now I was curious about how something could have blurred Val's vision but not her sense of smell. Something that didn't want people to see it coming and going, maybe, and didn't think that an animal would remember the scent trail later. Something that hadn't counted on a werewolf hanging around out back of Hillside High School on a Friday night.

I had an idea. I didn't like it very much, but if it worked, it would explain everything. I took off my backpack and opened it up.

"The moon hasn't been down more than two hours," I said. "You're closer now to what you were last night than you're going to be for another twenty-eight days."

She looked dubious. "So?"

"So you've told me before that enhanced sense of smell is the first part of the change to arrive, and the last to leave. I want you to sniff some things, and tell me if any of them smell like what you smelled last night."

Val knows the sort of stuff I carry in my backpack. That lame excuse for a good idea made her smile at me like I'd just come up with the Master Plan to Save the Universe. I tried to feel as clever as she seemed to think I was, and pulled a vial of yellow powder out of my backpack. I had to take my gloves off to unscrew the lid—childproof caps were never meant to be opened out-of-doors in January—before I handed the bottle to Val.

"Did it smell like that?"

Val waved her hand over the open bottle to bring the smell to her nose, the way they show you how to do it in chemistry class so that nobody takes a deep breath of something nasty and falls down choking. She sneezed a little, more of a snort, then wrinkled up her nose and handed the bottle back.

I screwed the lid back on. "Well?"

"No," she said. "Nothing like that."

"Good." That ruled out sulphur and brimstone, which was fine by me. Some problems are a bit bigger than I really want to deal with. "Okay. Let's try the next one."

So we worked our way, one thing at a time, through the rest of the stuff I lug around—rose petals, salt water, hydrochloric acid—everything but the garlic oil, for reasons that ought to be obvious. I was getting close to the bottom, and starting to think that maybe this hadn't been such a hot idea after all, when Val snorted again and said, "That's it."

I looked again at what I'd dragged up. It was a little aluminum-foil packet of red rowan berries. "You're sure?"

"Of course I'm sure."

Another piece of theory clicked into place. "Okay," I said. "I think I know what happened to Candi. But you're not going to believe it."

"Try me," Val said.

"She's gone off to Fairyland."

Val stared at me. "She's done *what?*"

It sounded even stupider now that I'd said it out loud than it had when I was thinking about it. But it was the only answer that fit.

"Fairyland," I said again, talking real fast before Val could start laughing. "You know, the good folk. The people of the hills. 'Up the airy mountain, down the rushy glen—'"

"'We daren't go a-hunting, for fear of little men,'" Val finished for me. We'd had the same teacher for third grade, and Mrs. Esterbrook had really loved that poem. "Like that?"

"Like that," I said. "And you remember how the rest of it goes, too."

Val nodded. "'They stole little Bridget, for seven years long, and when she came back, her friends were all gone.' That part always used to give me the creeps."

"Well," I said, "unless I miss my guess that's exactly what happened here. Candi's going to spend the night with this guy dancing and partying and having a good old time, and when she gets home in the morning she's going to find out that it's seven or twenty or a hundred years from now."

"And we're all dead of old age, there's a flying-saucer factory where the high school used to be, and she has absolutely no job skills." Val was looking *really*

170

worried now, and I braced myself for what I knew she was going to say next. "Freddie, we have to go help her."

"It looks from here like she went along of her own free will," I said. "That's not going to make it easy."

"Do you suppose that guy—whatever he was—explained it all to her?"

"No," I admitted. "He probably told her they were just going to a party, and like a damn fool she went."

"All right, then," Val said, as if that settled it. "You're the expert. How do we get her out?"

Expert . . . yeah, right. I thought hard and tried to look knowledgeable. "Well, there's two ways we could do it. One, we can wait a month for the next full moon, and spend the time from now to then doing our research and getting ready—"

"Or two, we can go now," Val said.

I wasn't surprised. Like I said, reckless.

"Right, then." I tried to pretend that I wasn't making all this up as I went along. I've read every word in the public library on occultism, the supernatural, folklore, and fairy tales, and about half the time it's useless. Make that more than half the time. The situation is really pathetic.

I opened my pack again and pulled out a ball of twine. I didn't know if I ought to be measuring it out in rods, meters, yards, furlongs, or cubits, so I just cut off a convenient length. After that it was straight geometry to inscribe a triangle around the patch of snow where the footprints had vanished. I used wooden pegs to anchor the three corners of the triangle: one of oak, one of ash, and one of bitter thorn.

171

Val just shook her head when I told her what they were. "I might have known you'd be carrying something like that."

"Hey, it pays to be prepared." Actually, it was more by good luck than good judgment that I'd had the stakes with me. I'd ordered them out of a specialty catalog at the same time I'd gotten the rowan berries.

Once the triangle was finished, I walked back a bit and sighted along the trail of hoofprints until I had one tree lined up ahead and another one behind. I cut more string and tied one end to the tree behind and the other end to the tree ahead, where the trail would have gone if the trail had gone anywhere. Then I was ready. I stuffed everything into my pack except for the rowan berries, and put it back on.

"Okay," I said to Val. "We're going to re-create last night and see what happens. Maybe there's a gate here, and maybe it's still open. You hold the string in your right hand, I hold it in my left, and we match our footsteps to the prints in the snow. And one more thing"— I spilled out some of the rowans into my hand—"hold these in your fist, next to your skin."

Val nodded, stripped off a glove, and took the berries.

I grabbed the string. "Ready?"

"Ready," said Val. She had the string in hand and was wearing her best scared-but-determined expression, the one that usually means she's about to go out looking for trouble instead of being sensible and waiting for it to show up. "Let's do it."

I fitted my boots into the track of the cloven hooves, and we stepped out. I tried to keep my mind a blank—

which is harder than it sounds like, especially if you're in the habit of thinking about things—while I fixed my eyes on the tree up ahead. I could tell when we crossed into the pegged-out triangle. It made my back teeth hurt, which I think was my mind interpreting a sensation that wasn't supposed to be physical in the first place; when I thought about the feeling hard enough to give it a name, it went away.

Then we were across the triangle, and over on the other side of the clearing. I thought for a moment that nothing had happened—except that I'd made myself look stupid, of course—and then I looked back the way we had come.

There was the string, and there was the triangle laid out and pegged down in the snow, but last night's wolf tracks weren't there at all—and the trail of Candi and Cloven-Hoof started again in the clearing and went on out into the trees.

Our own tracks led backward, to the center of the triangle, and no farther. Val looked around, her eyes very wide and sharp, and I heard her take a deep breath.

"Freddie," she said, "I don't think we're in Kansas anymore."

"We weren't in Kansas to start with."

"Freddie!"

"I know what you mean." I sealed my mail-order rowan berries back up in their tinfoil packet. No telling when I might need them again—on our way back, for sure. Which reminded me—one thing all the folktales agreed on: "This is important. Don't eat or drink *anything*. If you do, they own you."

"Me and Persephone," she said. Werewolves in

general have big appetites—the souped-up metabolism has to get its fuel from somewhere—and Val's no exception. "What happens if Candi's already hit the refreshment table?"

"Then we may be flat out of luck," I said. "Let's hope she's been too busy partying to go looking for a snack."

We started out again, following the tracks. They didn't go far before Cloven Hooves dropped down from two legs onto four. That's when I figured Candi got the hint. Her trail split off from his, and her stride lengthened out, like she was running. I saw the place where she tripped, her body landing in the snow. She used her hands to push herself up, and she started running again.

Then other footprints appeared, coming out of the woods—all different sizes, the bottoms of their shoes flat and smooth, not like the waffle-print winter boots Candi had been wearing. The new tracks converged on Candi and stopped her. Then Mr. Cloven Hooves trotted up alongside, and after that I couldn't find her footprints anymore.

"What do you think?" Val asked. She hadn't said anything since we'd left the clearing, but I could tell she was seeing it the same way I was.

"They put her on Goat-Guy, and she rode from here. So let's go. Daylight's burning."

Which was something else I needed to figure out. If one night in Fairyland equaled one hundred years on earth, then one minute here would equal nearly two months at home, which meant that if we headed back right now we'd show up sometime during summer vacation—and have a whole lot of explaining to do.

On the other hand— If that was really how the time thing worked, then we'd have shown up on this side only nanoseconds after Candi and Goat-Guy. So time passed normally here; you just didn't get old, and you were having so much fun you didn't notice.

Well, I wasn't having fun.

We followed the tracks in the snow, until we came to a place where the woods thinned out, and the snow vanished from the ground.

"End of the line," I said. "Can't track somebody where there's no trail."

If you want to know the truth, I was sort of relieved. Not having Candi to worry about meant I could put all my energy into worrying about getting home, because I didn't have a lot of confidence we could work the string trick twice. If back and forth to elfland was easy, everyone would be doing it. But I should have known Val wouldn't give up so easily.

"We don't have to track them," she said. "I can smell them. They're right around here."

Her voice sounded funny, and when I glanced over at her I saw why. Her face had changed, lengthening in the nose and jaw, not to mention growing fur and whiskers, and her canine teeth were longer than they ought to have been. If you want me to be honest about it, she had fangs—and between the too-sharp teeth, the too-long tongue, and the altered jawline, her diction was really shot.

I managed not to stare. Val's a pretty girl and she makes a handsome wolf, but as a general rule she's either all of one or all of the other—this half-and-half business was kind of grotesque by comparison.

Somehow, though, I didn't think she'd appreciate having me point that out.

"Over to you, then," I said. "Which way did they go?"

Her nose wrinkled as she sniffed the air. "That way. Not far."

She started off, and I followed. I tried to keep my mind clear, the way I had while we were following the string in the woods behind the school, and I guess it worked—I could feel when things changed, like I'd felt it when I crossed over the boundary back in the clearing. When I took my eyes off Val's red knit cap and looked around, we were there.

Or someplace, anyhow. It was still the woods in winter, with ice on the tree branches, even if the ground was bare; but it wasn't empty anymore. It was full of creatures—some of them almost human looking and some of them pretty close to animals, and some others half-and-half, like Val. Some of them had horns and some of them had hooves, and quite a few of them had fangs.

All of them were having a high old time. I couldn't tell where the music was coming from—the two or three creatures who seemed to be playing musical instruments couldn't possibly have accounted for all of the tones and harmonies by themselves—but it definitely had a beat you could dance to, because everybody was. Heck, I felt like tapping a foot to the rhythm myself.

And Candi was right in the middle of it. I have to admit something—up to that point I hadn't been real clear in my mind which of the girls in Val's homeroom we were supposed to be rescuing. Now that I'd seen her, I knew who she was, and if you want to know the truth, I wasn't surprised that I hadn't remembered her. Back in school, she'd been the sort of quiet, washed-out person who doesn't make much of an impression even when she's sitting right next to you. When a handsome stranger picked her up out of the crowd and promised her something a lot more exciting than crepe-paper streamers in the high school gym...She never had a chance.

But as Val would undoubtedly tell me if I brought the subject up, none of that mattered. Candi was human, and the rest of these people weren't, and they sure as heck hadn't laid out all their cards on the table at the start of the game.

If we were going to rescue her, though, we had our work cut out for us. She'd taken off her coat and her boots, and was dancing barefoot in her party dress on the freezing ground. And as for the expression on her face...some experiences have your everyday, consensus reality just plain outclassed, and it looked like she was having one of them.

"All right," I said to Val, "which of us gets to be the party pooper?"

Val didn't say anything. When I looked at her, I saw that her eyes were strange and bright, and she was starting to rock on her feet to the rhythm of the drums and pipes.

"Uh, Val..."

"Look at them," she said. "They're all like me."

"Not really," I said. "Werewolves are a real-world supernatural phenomenon. And in case you hadn't noticed—"

"—this isn't the real world? Sure looks real enough to me."

She started forward. I grabbed her by the arm. Val's strong; she pulled away from me and dashed into the dance. I stood there with my mouth open, feeling stupid, until somebody came up and took me by the hands.

It was a girl with bright yellow hair. "Come dance with me," she said. Her eyes were as golden as her hair. But when her tongue darted out for a second from between her lips, I saw that it was forked, like a snake's. *Not human,* I thought. *None of them are human except for me and Val and Candi*—and when I caught sight of Val again, she wasn't looking particularly human either.

"Sorry," I said to the snake girl. "Previous engagement." I dropped her hands and started pushing toward Candi through the press of dancers. I deliberately tried to ignore the beat of the music, but it sure was hard. Candi first, to see if I could reach her at all; and after Candi, Val.

When I reached Candi, at least she recognized me—it made me glad she didn't know I'd had trouble recalling her face. "Freddie!" she said, all happy smiles. "Isn't this an absolutely *wonderful* party?"

"Uh, yeah," I said. "We have to leave, though. It's time to go home."

"But I just got here!"

This wasn't working out very well. "Take a look around you. This isn't Earth. We're way out of place."

She didn't seem to have heard me. "Why don't you take off that backpack and jacket? We'll dance for a bit and we'll leave by morning, okay?"

"You'd better wake up," I told her. "It already *is* morning."

I don't think she heard me. But it didn't matter. Because right then, as I glanced out past Candi's shoulder, I saw Val. She stood at the edge of the dancing ground with a dark wooden cup in her hand, and it looked like she was getting ready to drink.

Sometimes you don't know what your priorities are until you see them in action. I left Candi behind without bothering to say so much as, "Sorry," and made it through the crowd of dancers in a panicky sprint. I'd like to say that I snatched the cup from Val's hand at the last moment . . . but the truth of the matter is, I skidded into her so hard that she dropped it.

Good enough, though. Whatever was in the cup spilled onto the ground, and Val grabbed me by both shoulders before I could fall on top of it. She looked more like a wolf than ever, and I think she had claws. She was snarling at me like a wolf, that was for sure.

"You did that on *purpose,* Freddie Hanger!"

"You're right!" I was close to yelling myself, and it wasn't just to make my voice heard over the music, either. "Didn't you hear what I told you—if you eat or drink anything in a place like this, you're stuck!"

Her eyes had gone greenish yellow, like a wolf's eyes. "Well, maybe I wanted to be stuck here, did you ever think of that?"

"I thought of it. I just didn't believe you'd be that stupid."

"It's not stupid," she said. "Look at me, Freddie. I'm not human—I'm one of them, or the next thing to it!"

"You're a human girl, and I love you." That shocked me. It was the first time I'd ever said anything about love to her. Val looked shocked, too, in a kind of wolfish way. But at least she was thinking about what I'd said, so maybe things weren't hopeless.

"Okay," I said. "I'm going to get out of here. Do you want to come or not?"

She gave herself a shake, like a dog throwing off rainwater, and said, "What about Candi?"

I glanced back the way I'd come. Candi was still out there dancing. I didn't know if I'd managed to get through to her or not. I still had that tinfoil packet of rowan berries in my pocket. I pulled the packet out and opened it.

Time stopped. And the dancers with it. The only ones moving were me and Val—and Candi. With the music gone, she looked cold and forlorn.

"What happened?" she asked.

"We're going home," I said. I gave Candi one of the rowan berries, and Val another, and kept a third one out for myself. "These should keep us safe until we're out of here. I don't know how long the effect will last, though, so let's start walking."

And we walked. Before long we were at the woods. Then at the tracks. Then at my triangle of string and pegs.

"Okay," I said. "Here's the drill. We hold rowan berries. We hold hands. We close our eyes and follow that line, straight through the center of the triangle."

Val looked uneasy—as uneasy as someone with a face halfway to lupine can manage to look, anyway. "What if I don't change back when we get out?"

"I don't think that's likely to be a problem," I said, trying to sound like I actually knew what would happen. "Either this works all the way or it doesn't work at all."

"Oh," Val said. "Maybe I should be thinking about a second career with the fairy people, just in case."

"No!" My voice came out a bit louder than I meant it to. "You have to stay clear on what you're doing with this stuff. There's no fudge factor built into it."

Candi was looking at the tracks in the snow as if she didn't remember making them. "Home," she said. She didn't sound real enthusiastic about it, either. "You said it was already morning back there?"

"That's right."

"Oh no. My parents are going to kill me—even if I don't tell them the truth."

She was probably right, at that. But waiting around for morale to improve wasn't going to get us anywhere. I passed out more rowan berries, and we joined hands—three together like the spokes of a wheel, so that each of us was holding hands with both of the others. I didn't want anybody hanging out alone at the end of the line.

"Okay," I said. "Here we go."

I matched my stride to the footprints I'd left before, closed my eyes, and stepped out. Through our clasped hands I could feel Val and Candi doing the same thing. One more time I tried not to think of anything at all, and one more time I felt myself pass through that barrier that wasn't there. It was harder going this time, as if we were moving against a current. The triangle felt two or three times bigger than it had when I first made it, and pushing my way across it made me break out in a sweat in spite of the cold.

Halfway across, one of the hands on mine pulled free. I couldn't tell whose it was, and I didn't dare open my eyes to look.

"We can't stop," I said. "If we stop, we'll never get home."

Nobody answered.

Then we were at the far edge of the triangle, and I felt us stepping through. I didn't want to open my eyes, but I did.

"Freddie?" said Val.

She had her own face again, and she was looking backward at the triangle in the snow. Nobody's footprints came out of it but ours. Candi was gone.

Val's face had the angry look she gets when she's too upset to cry. "All that trouble, and then she had to turn around and go back—!"

"Face it," I said. "Candi never wanted to leave in the first place. She looked like she was having more fun there than she ever did at home."

"*I* was having fun back there, too, and *I* didn't decide to trade in the real world for a hundred years or so of dancing all night with Mr. Goat Foot and his Fairyland pals!"

Maybe not, but she'd come close. I didn't think right now was the time to say that, though, because Val had left the party with me when I asked her to, and she hadn't looked back.

She was still plenty upset, though. She didn't say much of anything for most of the walk back to the parking lot.... She just trudged along through the snow with her hands in her pockets, scowling at last night's footprints all the way.

Finally she heaved a big sigh and said, "So what are we going to tell people when they ask us what happened?"

"Nobody's going to ask us about it," I said. "Neither one of us was at the dance, remember? If anybody thinks anything, they'll think that Candi walked over to the state highway and hitched a ride to the coast—with a family like hers, who'd be surprised? It happens all the time."

I was feeling a bit down by then myself, and it wasn't just the aftermath of a morning's adrenaline-charged adventuring, either. It was guilt. I'd been the one who talked to Candi—and I'd left her standing there flatfooted the moment I saw that Val was in trouble. And all I could think of when I came out of that triangle and opened my eyes was how glad I was that Val hadn't been the one who decided to stay behind.

Snow was starting to fall again.

By midday the tracks would be gone.

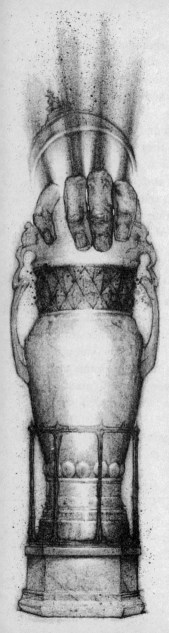

JANE YOLEN

BOLUNDEERS

The one chore Brancy hated more than any other was taking out the food scraps and emptying them into the compost heap. She didn't mind the dry garbage, or rinsing out the **bottles** and cans for the recycling bins. She didn't even mind tying up the endless numbers of newspapers that seemed to positively breed in her mother's den, though she refused to go into the den to get them. But the compost...

She flung the final bucketload onto the small mountain of scraps and tried not to watch the tomato ends and eggshells creep down the slimy sides. And she didn't take a new breath until she was well upwind and moving fast.

God! she thought. Then amended it quickly, in case God was listening, though she doubted He was. *Gosh!* Ever since her father's death she had had these big moments of Unbelief. *Still,* she thought, *probably better not to swear.* She had an additional thought then. *Imagine if the whole world was like the compost heap. And not just my life.*

Of course, the world had once actually been that way. They had talked about that in school. The Cretaceous, with its great, wet, green, muddy, mucky, swamp-and-romp dinosaur playground. It was supposed to have been full of fetid and moist, murky growth. Like an overgrown compost heap. *Imagine living in that!* Brancy thought. *I'd rather die first.*

The word *die* resounded inside her. It was ugly and sharp and it hurt.

She rinsed the pail at the outside tap, then walked back into the house. "Done," she called out to her little brother. "I get dishes tomorrow and you, Mr. Brat—you get the compost."

"I hate the compost," Danny whimpered. "Something's growing out there." He spoke in the quiet, whispery, scared voice he had used ever since their father died.

"Of course something's growing there," Brancy said. She deliberately made her voice sound spooky.

"It is?" His eyes got wide.

"Volunteers," Brancy told him. "And if you're not careful, they'll get you!"

"Mommmmmmmy," Danny cried, and ran out of the room.

Moments later he came back, followed by their mother. She was not amused. "Brancy, he has had enough nightmares since...without you adding to them." Her mother never actually used the word *death*. Or *cancer*. Her conversation was full of odd ellipses and gaps. Brancy hated it. "I need you to be more...understanding about...about things."

"All I said was that volunteers grow up in the compost heap. And you know they do."

"She said the Bolundeers would get me." Danny was white faced. "Maybe get all of us. Like they got..." He didn't say the word *Daddy*. He didn't have to.

Mrs. Callanish knelt down. "Oh, Danny, a *volunteer*"—she pronounced the word very carefully—"is a tomato or squash or some other vegetable that grows from the seeds that are thrown into the compost heap. And they can't possibly get you. Not like...Have you ever seen a fierce tomato or a mean pumpkin?" She made a face.

"At Halloween," Brancy said. "All those teeth."

"Brancy!" Mrs. Callanish's mouth was drawn down into a thin line.

Brancy knew, even before her mother spoke, that she had gone too far this time. In fact, since her father's death everything that Brancy said or did seemed wrong, hurtful, awry.

Her mother was changed, too, beyond all recognition. Before, she had been a funny, cozy kind of mom, always ready to listen, even when she was busy. And as a DA, she was always busy. Now she was stern and unreachable. Brancy understood why—or thought she did. Her mother was trying to be brave and strong, like her father had been throughout his illness. But what made everything worse was that her mother never let them talk about him. About his illness, about his death. She just set his memory firmly between the spaces. He was . . . (gone). . . . It was almost as though he had never been a part of their lives at all.

"Okay, get your homework out of the way and then we can have a chapter of Tolkien tonight. I've managed to get most of my work done." Mrs. Callanish nodded, but there was no warmth in her voice, as if reading to them were a duty she was still willing to perform—but not one she was happy doing.

Brancy knew that Danny would be finished with his homework first. After all, how much homework does a kindergartner have, except maybe coloring? But she had at least an hour of math and social studies and a whole page of spelling words to memorize. Mr. Dooley, her English teacher, was a bear on spelling words. He had won a national spelling bee as a fourth grader and loved to tell them about it. Before her father had died, Brancy had been class champion—and Mr. Dooley's pet. But she had gotten Cs on her last three spelling tests and had never made up the two she missed because of the funeral. Mr. Dooley didn't even kid around with her anymore. *Which is fine,* Brancy thought. *Just fine. Mr. Dooley is kind of goofy on the subject of spelling anyway.*

———

It turned out to be more like three hours of homework, though—one before the Tolkien, and two after—and Brancy was exhausted. Eighth grade was going to be real hard, she decided. The spelling words had been the worst ever: *naiad, Gorgon, nemesis, daimonic, centaur, odyssey.* They were studying the myths of ancient worlds. Brancy wished the ancient worlds had known how to spell with more regularity. Or had fewer odd gods and monsters.

"Though how anyone could *really* believe in this stuff..." she said, slamming the book shut. "It's all too bizarre."

"Brancy," came a whispery voice from the door connecting her bedroom with Danny's.

She looked up. Danny was standing there, holding on to his bear, Bronco.

"Hey, Mr. Brat, it's way past ten. What are you doing up?"

"I heard the Bolundeers outside. In the compost." His chin trembled. "They're scratching around. And whispering awful things about you and me and Mom. They want to come into the house. Listen."

She listened. All she could hear were crickets. "You know what Mom said. *Volunteers*"—she pronounced it carefully, "are vegetables. And vegetables don't make any noise. In fact, they are very very quiet."

"Not these ones," Danny said. "These are Bolundeers. They want to hurt us. Brancy, I'm scared."

She started to say something sharp but his face was so pinched and white that she bit back the response. He hardly looked like a kindergartner anymore. In fact, he looked like a little old man. A little old *dying* man. "Do

188

you want me to snuggle with you till you fall asleep?"

He nodded, clutching Bronco so hard the little bear's eyes almost popped out.

"Okay. I was getting tired of Gorgons and centaurs anyway."

"What are those?"

"Far worse than talking veggies, trust me." She followed him back to his bed. Tucking in next to him, she said, "Why don't I sing you something?" He nodded, and so she started with their father's favorite lullaby, the one he always sang when they were sick and couldn't fall asleep: "Dance to Your Daddy." Only, unlike their father, she sang it on key.

Danny dozed off at once, but Brancy could not sleep. The song only served to remind her that her father was no longer around. He had suffered horribly before finally dying, and God had been no help to him at all. Even though they had all prayed and his partner had had a mass said for him. It didn't matter that her father had been strong and brave before he had gotten cancer. With medals from the city after having been injured in the line of duty. He hadn't died when some man crazy with drugs had tried to kill him with a knife. Or later, when he had shielded two hostages with his own body while a would-be burglar had shot at them. It was stupid lung cancer from his stupid smoking that had killed him. She tried to remember what her father had looked like, either before the cancer or after. But all that came to mind was what they had left of him, in a jar on a shelf in her mother's den.

Ashes.

Morning was dirty and gray as an erased black-board. Brancy got up from her brother's bed, where she had slept fitfully, on top of the covers. She brushed her teeth quickly, ran her fingers through her short hair, and got dressed with a lack of enthusiasm. The other girls in her class, she knew, made dressing the long, important focus of their day. But ever since... She stopped herself. Then, afraid that she was beginning to sound like her mother, she said aloud, "Ever since Daddy died..." Well, clothes and things weren't so important anymore. Or school.

In fact, Brancy was so tired, she dozed through most of her classes. She was all but sleepwalking when she picked up Danny from afternoon kindergarten. Still, she was awake enough to see that his pinched-old-man look was gone, and she smiled at him. Hand-in-hand they walked back toward home, with Danny babbling on and on about stuff in a normal tone. Only when they turned the corner of Prospect Street, he was suddenly silent and his face was the gray-white of old snow.

"Cat got your tongue, Mr. Brat?" Brancy asked.

"Do you think..." he whispered, "that the Bolun-deers will be waiting for us?"

"Oh, Danny!" Brancy answered, unable to keep the exasperation in her voice hidden. She was too tired for that. "Mom explained. I explained." She shook her head at him. But his hand in hers was damp.

"Don't let them get me, Brancy," he said. "Don't let them hurt me. I'm not brave like Daddy."

She dropped his hand and knelt down in front of him so they were eye-to-eye. "No one," she said force-fully, "is going to hurt you. Not while I'm around."

"Daddy got hurt." His eyes teared up.

She dropped her books to the ground and put her arms around him. She couldn't think of anything to say. And besides, their mother didn't want them to talk about it. She found herself snuffling, and Danny pulled away.

"Don't cry, Brancy," he said.

"I'm not crying. I've got a rain cloud in my eyes." It was something their father use to say.

"Oh, Brancy!" Danny was suddenly bright again, as if he had forgotten all about his fears. He took her hand. "I think we need to go home now."

And they did. Straight home. Without talking.

Brancy did her homework in the living room, to keep an eye on Danny while he watched television. But she was so engrossed in the reading she didn't notice when he left the room in between commercials. When she realized he was gone, she got up, stretched, and went to look for him.

He wasn't downstairs, and she raced up the stairs to see if he was—for some reason—in the bedrooms. Sometimes, she knew, a five-year-old could get into a lot of trouble by himself. But he wasn't upstairs, either. She was close to panic when she glanced out the bedroom window and saw him by the compost heap. What he was doing there was so shocking, she screamed. Then she ran down the stairs and outside, without taking time to put her shoes on. The grass soaked her socks.

"Danny!" she cried. "Stop! Oh, Danny. What have you done?"

He turned to her, smiling. "Daddy will take care of those Bolundeers all right. Just like he takes care of all the bad guys."

She took the urn from him and looked in. It was totally empty. She didn't dare stare over his shoulder into the compost heap, where she knew the gray ashes would already be settling into the slime. "Oh, Danny," she whispered, "we can't tell Mommy. We just can't."

And they didn't. Not at dinner, and not at bedtime. Danny because he'd promised Brancy, and he did not know exactly what was wrong. And Brancy because she did know. Exactly.

That night, as she lay in her bed, Brancy heard the sound Danny must have been listening to the night before. The crickets, of course. But underneath their insistent high-pitched chirrupings, something else. Something odd and ugly, scratching and scrabbling across the grass. It sounded awkward and eager, as if it had gained strength before judgment, as if it were hungry, as if it were heading toward the house.

Brancy got up and looked out of the window, but she couldn't see anything out there. Except a series of strange flat black shapes that seemed to hunch and bunch through the grass. But the moon was full and the lawn was covered with shadows. Surely that was what she was seeing.

She shut her window as quietly as possible and pulled down the shade. Then she crept into Danny's room, her heart thudding so loudly she thought it would wake her mother down the hall.

Danny was clutching his bear as if he were frightened, but he was fast asleep. Brancy lay down next to him, afraid to think, afraid to move again, afraid to breathe.

The strange scratching, scrabbling sound seemed to come closer, reaching below Danny's window. Brancy forced herself to get up, to go over to the window and shut it. It slammed down on the sill with a loud *whack* as sharp as gunshot. But not before she saw the shadows rising up, like some sort of anonymous and deadly gang, their shadowy fingers pointing at her, their shadowy mouths calling in voices as soft and persuasive as dreams. "Danny . . . we're coming for you next!"

"No!" she cried out loud, "not Danny." She flung herself back onto the bed, setting herself over Danny to protect him. She could feel him breathing beneath her, gentle and trusting; her own breathing was a harsh rasp.

And then she heard something else. It was faint, so faint that at first she thought she was only wishing it. But it got louder, as if whatever made that particular noise had come closer, or had gained its own particular strength from her. It was—she thought—a sound that was strangely off-key. But she recognized it. It was a song, and she sang along with it, quietly at the beginning, then with growing gusto: "Dance to your daddy, my little laddy . . ."

Danny stirred in his sleep and nuzzled the bear.

"Brancy?" Her mother's voice floated down the hall.

Brancy stopped singing just long enough to call back: "Under control, Mom."

The song seemed to catch up with the eager scratching, then overtake it. There was a moment of strange cacophony, like some kind of grunge band suddenly playing beneath their window.

And then, as if it had been a vine cut down, the scratching stopped.

Slowly the off-key song faded away, and all she could hear then were the ever-present crickets and the faraway hooting of a screech owl, like a lost child crying in the distance.

Brancy got up, went to the window, and slowly raised it. The air was soft and a shred of cloud covered the full moon. She thought it might soon rain.

"I love you, Daddy," Brancy whispered to the lawn and, beyond it, the compost heap. Then she closed her eyes, which rain-clouded over with tears. "I miss you." She went back to her own bedroom and lay down on the bed. A minute later she felt someone lift the covers up and over her and hum a bit of an off-key tune.

She didn't open her eyes to see who it was.

She didn't have to.

The next morning at breakfast, Mrs. Callanish stood by the table looking stern, the urn in her arms.

Brancy started to say something, but her mother shook her head.

"I had the most amazing dream last night," she said. "About your...father." She took a deep breath. "I've been wrong to keep his ashes hidden in my den. To make a shrine of them. To forbid you to talk about him and how he died."

Brancy took a deep breath, this time determined to confess what had happened.

But her mother continued talking. "Let's go and spread the ashes in the garden. It was his favorite place. He'll like being there."

"But ..." Brancy began, then she looked over at Danny. He was smiling. It was a secret, knowing kind of smile.

Suddenly she understood. The ashes—which she had seen him shake out onto the compost heap—were somehow back in the urn. And then she remembered the soft touch of the shadowy hand on her covers, the soft off-key humming above her bed.

"We can sing Daddy's song while we do it," Danny said. "About dancing."

"I didn't know you knew it," Mrs. Callanish said.

"I know it all," Danny said.

"And what you forget," Brancy added, "I'll remember."

NANCY SPRINGER

YEAH, YEAH

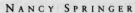

Jessie put on her brother's T-shirt. He was dead. She put on his blue pullover sweater. He had been dead for a week, and it was her fault. She put on his jeans—they fit pretty well. He had been a year younger, a few inches taller. She put on his tube socks and his Adidas. They were only half a size too large. She could wear them.

With a pair of scissors Jessie went to the bathroom

mirror. Hack, hack, hack, with a quick, firm hand. Chunks of hair clotted the sink till all the perm had fallen away and only a lank draggle remained. The style, or lack of any, was right and so was the color, dusky blond. People had always said she and her brother looked alike.

She missed him so much. Her loudmouthed kid brother, the lord of the Cantrell family. Dead.

She wore no makeup or jewelry or perfume. Hadn't worn any since the day he died, not even to the funeral. But she had kept eating, at least. Her mother had not been eating.

Her mother had not spoken to her since it happened. Not one word.

Jessie left the scissors where she had laid them, the way her brother would have. She left the hair in the sink, thumped down the stairs, and strode into the kitchen, swaggering a little, the way a certain bumptious boy would have. "Yo, Mudder," she said in a deep voice to the woman sitting listlessly at the table.

Her mother jerked upright and gawked. Then her mouth closed and curled into a soft Mona Lisa smile. "Well, hi, Jeremy," she whispered. "How's my boy?" A single tear slipped down from her left eye.

Jessie's chest heaved with relief. She hugged her mother around the shoulders. Her mother's hand came up to pat her head.

"Don't forget your lunch money," her mother said.

"Yeah, yeah," Jessie said, the way Jeremy would have. "See ya, Mud." She barged out the door, heading for school.

———

"You're sick," her best friend, Kiesha, whispered to her at lunchtime. People, including teachers, had been trying to laugh off her Jeremy imitation, but now they were starting to get upset.

"Yeah, yeah."

"Stop it, Jessie! Talk like yourself."

Jessie sighed. "What self is that?" But, sitting next to Kiesha, she found herself talking in her normal quiet Jessie voice, being the studious, mousy Cantrell, the invisible one who never talked back or had a date. "I don't have a self. Ask anybody. Jessie who? My mother's been looking right through me."

"Your mother? Why?"

"She—she blames me for what happened."

"That's not fair. It's not your fault."

Jessie's emotions veered. "But I should have been in the car with him." She needed to defend her mother. "I should have been driving." She needed her own guilt to keep her going. "I should have been the one who died."

"Bull. You didn't do anything. You didn't tell Jeremy to wreck."

Jessie shook her head, shaking away the words like a colt shaking away flies. It was rude and selfish to blame the dead. Blame Jeremy? But he had just been acting like a boy. She was the big sister and the one who had the driver's license and the one who had borrowed the Mustang; she should have taken responsibility. Not that anyone was thinking she shouldn't have let Jeremy drive; probably not even her mother was thinking that. Jeremy was the Crown Prince of Cantrell; Mom had always given him whatever he wanted, especially since Dad had split. But when he had started speeding, Jessie should have sweet-talked him into slowing down. She should have whimpered that she was scared. She should have coaxed and begged.

Instead, she had ordered him. And he had told her to shut up. And she had not shut up. And he had screeched to a messy stop and told her to get out. And she had gotten out, never expecting him to drive away and leave her.

And somewhere down the dark road, the curve and the ditch and the impassive oak trees had taken him.

"I should have stayed with him," she said.

"And gotten yourself killed?"

"I should have."

"Is that why you're wearing his clothes?"

This was getting annoying. "I can wear what I want. There's no law—"

"Jessie, how long are you going to keep this up?"

"As long as I damn well like!" She stood up and walked away with a boyish stride, her shoulders high and hard.

For supper that evening her mother made chicken cacciatore, Jeremy's favorite. Jessie went along with it. Her mom was smiling. Her mom was eating. Her mom was talking to her. "How was school?"

Jessie grunted.

"Didn't you have wrestling practice today?"

"Nah." Wrestling? Jessie felt a jolt of panic—this was supposed to be a game, a clown act, and Mom was supposed to understand that it was she, Jessie, who was trying to help her feel better. She did understand, right? Quickly, in her own voice Jessie said, "I got an *A* on a geometry quiz." Jeremy took algebra, not geometry. Jeremy never got an *A*.

Her mother's smile seeped away. Her mother stopped talking.

That night Jessie couldn't sleep. It felt like there was a stone the size of her clenched fists inhabiting her chest. At one in the morning she erupted out of bed, yanked on Jeremy's clothes because they were handy, and left the house, careful not to awaken her mother, treading quietly for a person in oversized Adidas. Under a cloudy moon she hiked the two miles to the cemetery. Jeremy's grave lay as raw as a recent laceration, even in the muted light. Jessie sat down on the dirt and cried.

"I—can't—stand—it," she sobbed to the night. She pounded the red earth of the mound with her hands, but then made herself stop. It wasn't his fault that she was remembering how he had teased her by hiding her homework, he had raced her for the bathroom in the morning and usually won, he had dared her to sneak into R-rated movies with him, he had talked Mom into letting her go to a dance when she was supposed to be grounded. It wasn't his fault that he had been brash and beautiful and now he was dead.

A sense of his sardonic presence settled on her like a mist, calming her. "Jeremy," she whispered.

Chill out, Sis, for God's sake.

"I can't. Mom is—Mom's a mess. She adored you." Mom had revolved around her boy like a satellite around the sun. "She worshiped you."

So what else is new?

"She never loved me that way."

Yeah, yeah.

200

Jessie got home about three in the morning, lay down in Jeremy's bed instead of her own, and was suddenly able to sleep. Walking into school late the next morning, she wore a Nirvana T-shirt, Levi's, a bomber jacket—Jeremy's clothes.

"This is not normal behavior, Jessica," the school psychologist intoned.

Rage careered through Jessie like a hot car out of control. She had never felt so angrily rebellious before. The pompous administrative dork—he said she was crazy just for wearing what she wanted to? Fine. She'd be crazy. "That's not my name," she said loudly. "Jeremy. Call me Jeremy."

"We all have to deal with reality, Jessie—"

She could use whatever name she wanted to. There was no law. "Call me *Jeremy*."

When he finally let her go back to class, she started putting her name on her papers that way. Jeremy Cantrell. It looked funny in her tidy, oval handwriting instead of his wild scrawl.

That night she lay down on his bed and slept at once, deeply and restfully, as she dreamed of him. She saw his proud teenage face as vividly as if he sat in the room with her. She saw his million-dollar grin. *Way to go, Sis.* She saw him give her a thumbs-up. He didn't look like a dead person.

She awoke feeling different. Better.

Her mother made her corn pancakes for breakfast. Jeremy's favorite. Hers too, now. Her mother smiled and reached across the table to stroke her face. "Son," she said tenderly, "you're growing up. You're going to have to start shaving soon."

Jessie lifted her hand. Felt the soft stubble beginning on her chin. Left the house in a daze. Her mother smiled and playfully swatted her rump, or the rump of Jeremy's jeans, sending her out the door.

Kiesha was crossing the parking lot as Jessie got out of her car. Lifting a hand to wave, Kiesha stopped dead and stared at her. Kiesha's hand sank like a dead thing. "My God," she said shakily. "Jessie, go someplace, now, this minute. Get away before it's too late."

And Jessie knew exactly what she meant. Yet out of her mouth Jeremy's deeper voice said, "Why should I?"

"Please," Kiesha whispered. There she stood, Jessie's best friend, tears in her eyes, yet Jessie did not seem able to connect. *Great hooters,* she thought. *Look at the hooters on her.* She had never thought such a thing before. She turned away.

Almost the minute she got to homeroom she was called to the office. The principal was waiting at the attendance desk to see her. "Jessica Cantrell," he told her, "we cannot have you representing yourself as Jeremy on school documents. It compromises the record keeping."

"I am Jeremy," she said.

"Nonsense." But the principal looked at her doubtfully. "Jeremy's name was withdrawn due to morbidity." But he frowned and glanced at a pale-faced, gawking secretary. She pulled out a file drawer and started shuffling through some manila cards. She stared. Then she trotted to her computer and clattered out something on the keys. Stared again at the data on the terminal.

In a voice like a stretched rubber band she told Jessie, "Excuse us a moment."

Jessie left. In the corridor she ran into some of Jeremy's wrestling buddies. "Hey, dude!" They lit up with grins, strutted, puffed their chests, punched her shoulders, which were big and strong enough to take it—when had she become so tall, so strong? Jeremy's Adidas fit her. His jeans hugged her, yet she felt slim and limber inside them.

Behind her in the office an administrative voice was yelling, "I don't care what the system says, the Cantrell boy died! We can't all go crazy."

"How'd you do it?" one of Jeremy's buddies asked. Though showing their teeth, they seemed unsurprised.

"Used a girl."

"Cool, man, that's what they're for."

A gray-suited administrator of some sort—the superintendent?—poked his head through the office doorway. "Jessica?"

"Jeremy."

"*Ms.* Cantrell, you are excused for the day. Till we get this straightened out. Sign this release slip and go home."

She scrawled JEREMY CANTRELL in a bold, messy hand and turned toward the door. "Way to go, dude!" her wrestling buddies called after her.

"*Hi,* Jeremy," said a smiling girl as she strutted out. Jessie knew her: one of the very popular girls. The boys flirted to her face, smirked behind her back, and called her the Golden Hind. She had never said hi to Jessie. Aside from Kiesha, none of the popular girls had ever said much to Jessie. But they all seemed to have a smile for Jeremy.

Kiesha was still standing in exactly the same place, crying, when Jessie swaggered back to the parking lot.

"Yo, babe, you wanna go somewhere?"

"Jessie!" Kiesha cried out as if somebody were dying. "Try to get away! Try!"

Love those hooters, Jeremy thought, right inside Jessie's head.

What were girls for? To be used?

She didn't want Jeremy thinking of Kiesha that way. It took a tremendous effort, but Jessie said something to Kiesha in her own voice. "I'm okay." She struggled to explain. "This is nice." Being Jeremy was great. Being a boy was great. She had never in her life felt so bold and strong and muscled and unworried. She had never felt so *cool.* It was like being a hero to have kids saying hi to her, Mom fluttering around and smiling and making her the center of the Cantrell universe. It was like being a hero, that she had been able to do this thing, to give Jeremy back to her mother.

"It's horrible," Kiesha whispered. "It's sick."

Jessie shrugged, got into her car, and jackrabbited out of there, screeching around corners all the way home. Not that there was any hurry. She just liked the adrenaline rush of driving fast.

Or rather, Jeremy liked it.

Jessie's mother was on the phone when she walked into the kitchen. Mom smiled and muffled the receiver with her hand. "It's the school," she stage-whispered.

"Some kind of mixup." She uncovered the receiver. "Yes, it has been a very difficult time," she said in dignified response to someone's apologies. "Please let your records show that I've lost a daughter." She said this with mild, moist-eyed regret, then lifted her head. "But I still have my wonderful son."

Jessie stood like stone, a carved graveyard angel. "I'm not dead," she protested, but she could not seem to speak loudly enough; her mother did not hear her.

She remembered Kiesha's horrified face. And—it felt like glass breaking, earth quaking, her bones cracking—she knew, she understood: She was not dead, but—she was not alive. She had thought she was being Jeremy, but—wrong. Jeremy was being Jeremy.

In her. Possessing her. He was far more alive than she could be, she who had never had a life. He was far stronger. She felt his cool presence flowing dark as cola in her veins. She flexed the smooth, hard muscle of his egotism. His uncomplicated self-will filled her now. His sheer and total sense of entitlement—she was no match. She had lost herself in love of him.

Yeah, yeah. So what else is new?

But she had never expected—she had not understood—always before they had been divided by their skins, but now she thought his thoughts, felt his feelings. Always before there had been her adoration to shield her. But now there was no way for her not to face his opinion of her.

Stupid. Loser. My sister, the dumb dog.

Her mother hung up the phone and lilted up the stairs, humming. Jessie tore lose from her stony stance and pounded after her.

But she froze again outside the door of her room. Mom was busy in there, cleaning, packing up her clothes and stuffed animals and hair scrunchies and posters and mall jewelry and fuzzy slippers, putting everything away.

"Mom," Jessie begged. "Mother. Please." *Please see me, please speak to me, Jessie, your daughter. Please*—but she couldn't say the word *love.* And her voice barely carried at all. Her mother didn't hear her.

She spun around and lunged into the bathroom, to the mirror. "I will get you," she whispered to Jeremy's handsome, mocking face looking back at her. "I'm somebody, dammit. I'm not done yet. *I'm not dead.*"

"Shut up." Jeremy's voice took over for good. "You're nothing. Always were. Right this minute they're putting up a grave marker with your name on it. You're nothing and you're always gonna be nothing."

She struggled but could not speak. He was too strong. She had said her last words with that mouth, those lips.

But her last words had spoken the truth. She was somebody. She was not dead. She was not finished.

Somehow in eternity I will get you.

Jeremy smiled. "Yeah, yeah."

SHERWOOD SMITH

ILLUMINATION

"Yo, Anna."

The wind rustling the winter-dry branches outside my window almost masked Ben's whisper.

"Ready to see the ghosts in Neverland?"

His voice was low, but I could hear the challenge. He didn't expect me to go. He didn't expect me to believe him.

"Sure," I said, and scrambled out my bedroom

window onto a branch and dropped to the grass.

We ran through the deserted streets of downtown. Neither of us spoke until we were almost to Neverland Park. Then Ben said, "We'd better hide."

He still expected me to scoff—or to run back home. I shrugged.

Even in the dark, I could see his surprise. Like ghosts playing in the town park wasn't as strange as the two of us being outside together at midnight, Ben—the school's bad kid—and me, Anna, the best student in school.

Ex-best student.

"Here's where," he said as we pounded across the grass toward a line of thick shrubs. Leaves skittered behind us down the pathway, driven by the chilly wind that numbed my lips and made my eyes water. I crouched beside Ben in the bushes.

"There they are," he said, staring across the playground, his breath making a faint glowing cloud.

We have the best park in five counties, designed and built by someone who grew up here, went away and made it rich, then came back old. Neverland Park was meant to be the closest thing to Peter Pan's island you could get on Earth—a place where kids could play forever.

Swinging from the ropes and twirling on the carousel and climbing all over the ladder-slide were about twenty kids. At first I thought Ben and those kids were scamming me, but then I noticed some things. Weird things. Like breathing. Ben's and my breath made clouds that glowed in the arc light reflections, and we were just sitting there. Those kids were all playing, some of them with their mouths open, but I didn't see anyone's breath.

And then there were the clothes. Oh, most of them looked like kids' anywhere—jeans, T-shirts, crummy shoes. But one girl on the swings wore a pinafore like straight out of *Little Women,* her long curls bouncing on her back as she kicked her feet. And walking along the top of the monkey bars was a boy in knee pants and a loose shirt like in *Tom Sawyer.*

"Ghosts," Ben said, with a strange kind of satisfaction.

I sucked in a long breath, and the cold made my lungs hurt. "Where d'you think they come from? And why are they *here*?"

Ben snorted. "They're from wherever ghosts come from. If I was a ghost I'd rather mess around at Neverland than hang out alone at some old house just to haunt it, wouldn't you? Twenty bucks," he added matter-of-factly, sticking out his hand.

I don't think he believed I'd pay up on the bet, either, because his eyes went wide with surprise when I yanked a crumpled bill from my jeans pocket and slapped it into his hand.

His mouth went sour. "You've got lots of twenties lying around?"

"In my mom's purse," I said. "Where I stole that from."

He snickered and turned to watch the kids playing again.

We watched for a little while longer, until my feet were numb and my fingers and nose ached. Then Ben turned to look at me, his narrowed eyes so steady I could see the bouncing, running ghost kids reflected in them. "What are you going to tell them at school?" he asked.

"Nothing," I said. "They can make their own bets."

He shrugged, backed out of the bush, and stood up. I followed, and again we were silent as we ran back toward my house.

When we reached my street we both stood there, breathing raggedly, then he said, "Want to watch 'em again tomorrow?"

"Sure," I said.

He ran off. I climbed back inside my room. Had my mother noticed I was gone?

I stood still, listening.

Nothing.

Next day at school in math class, my eyes itched and I kept yawning. Though Ben sat two rows away, I never looked at him. He must have been yawning, too, because he got yelled at twice for it.

In English, I guess he put his head down on his desk just after I did, because the teacher stopped talking and said sharply, "Benjamin, if you need to sleep, you may explain why to the vice principal. Now."

He got up. The teacher glared at him but never looked at me.

I closed my eyes, and the next thing I knew the bell had rung.

That night I set my alarm, because I knew I wouldn't be able to stay awake otherwise. I put it under my pillow, then turned off my light and lay back. The streetlight shone through tree branches, making shadows on my ceiling like bent witch fingers clawing up the walls.

I almost wanted to open my door, to call to Mom, but I heard the clink of dishes and her laughter. And *his* laughter.

I buried my face under the pillow and pressed my cheek against the clock, and listened to its ticking until I went to sleep.

"It's about time," I said when I saw Ben coming slowly up the sidewalk.

I was sitting on the lowest branch of the tree, swinging my feet. I'd planned it out—thought it'd look pretty cool if I was out there waiting, like I'd been there all night.

Ben shrugged, his bony shoulders jerking up and down. The shadows from the street lamp were odd on his face—made it look lopsided.

"Ready to run?" I asked, swinging to the ground.

"Nah," he said, kind of sarcastic. "What's the big hurry?"

I shrugged, making my shoulders jerk up and down. We walked.

When we neared the park, Ben said suddenly, "Let's go out there."

"You mean, let them see us?"

"Sure." He laughed, an angry snort of a laugh. "Why not? They're ghosts. Are you gonna get scared if they jump and yell 'Boo'?"

I said, as carelessly as I could, "Not sure being touched by a ghost is on my all-time want list."

"Like they can really hurt you," he sneered, and without waiting for me he launched straight across the grass toward the ghosts.

I hesitated, wondering what could happen to me.... If anything did, my mother wouldn't be alone at home when the phone rang. A big wash of anger burned away all my fear. I stumbled after Ben, my heart drumming loudly in my ears.

Ben was right in the middle of the park by then. At first it seemed the ghosts couldn't see him after all, but then they stopped what they were doing, first one or two, then four or five, then all of them. They stood, still and silent, their outlines glowing a kind of shivery silver and blue.

They moved toward us until they stood in a circle. I noticed odd things: that glow, and the fact that their feet didn't make prints in the sand, yet the cold winter wind ruffled their clothes and hair, same as ours. Their eyes were all dark.

"Hey! Can ya hear us?" Ben yelled, making me jump. He waved his arms and stamped toward a group of them.

At once they all started moving, some also waving their arms and stamping, and some clapping, and some twirling around in a kind of dance. Their mouths were open, like they were laughing, but the sound I heard was the wind rustling the barren twigs of the park trees.

Then flickering lights made us both duck. We looked up at the Main Street bridge arcing over the stream that runs through the park. Headlights jittered between the tree trunks lining the bridge.

"They can't see us down here," I said. My hands and lips were numb.

Ben stood very still, one hand gripping the opposite shoulder, then he turned away. "Let's go."

". . . and the article says that if you can talk to the spirit, you're supposed to ask if it can see the light," I said the next night.

My breath was puffing—this time Ben wanted to run. *At least we'll stay warm,* I thought.

"What light?" He turned and squinted at me. Those shadows were still on his face, and they hadn't moved. "Streetlights? Store lights?"

"I don't know," I said. "It just said 'light'—and you're supposed to tell them to go toward it. What is that on your face? Bruises?"

"I fall down a lot," he said. "So sue me. That 'light' stuff sounds like a load of garbage."

I snorted. "That's what I thought. Hanging out in the dark is cool—that's what I'd do if I was a ghost. But that's what it said in the encyclopedia."

"Why waste time reading that junk?" he snarled.

"You're sure in a good mood," I snarled back. "Anyway, it was better than yawning over that covalency grunge in the science book."

Ben snorted. "Old Man Mattson let you read during class?"

"He ignored me like I wasn't there," I said.

He shook his head. "Geez. Some people have all the luck. I drop a pencil on my desk, and he gives me an hour of detention. I miss an assignment, and I get sent to the VP."

"I haven't handed in any work for a week," I said, grinning. "All the teachers act like I'm still their perfect little super-student."

"Geez." Ben shook his head again.

We reached the park, and it looked like the ghosts were waiting for us. Only, there were more of them—maybe forty. As soon as we appeared, they all ran toward us. The grass waved in the cold wind—I could see it through their feet.

Then I was surrounded by them. Mostly girls, some of them hopping and dancing. The one in the pinafore was there, her wide eyes staring and staring. She reminded me a lot of my cousin Sarah, except this ghost was skinnier, and a couple years younger, and Sarah wasn't dead. The others pressed close, though not close enough to touch.

I walked slowly forward, and the ones in front backed away. We ended up at the swings, and for a time there I was, pumping high, with ghosts on either side of me, blown back and forth by the wind.

The ghost that reminded me of Sarah was on the next swing, her solemn little face angled my way, as though she were listening. Remembering what I'd read about the lights, I wondered if I should try to talk to her, but it seemed so stupid. If she couldn't see the streetlights as plainly as I could, what good would asking do? And what if it *did* somehow make her disappear? She was cute and fun to watch—I didn't want her to go.

I thought about asking Ben, and looked around, and realized I was alone except for the ghosts.

Ben wasn't in the park at all, but running with a

big swarm of ghosts up the steep embankment to the bridge.

Swinging high, I caught a glimpse of them through the trees sheltering the bridge. Then I heard brakes squealing.

My crowd of ghosts all drifted toward the carousel, looking back at me. Sarah hopped from one foot to the other, her bare feet passing through the sand. It looked weird, and I laughed. The ghosts all laughed as well— their mouths round and wide and dark.

Then we were on the carousel. The cold metal burned my hands, so I rubbed them together, then pushed with all my strength. The ghosts all piled on and we went around and around, the winter wind streaming through my hair and their bodies.

When Ben reappeared, I jumped down reluctantly, though my teeth were chattering again. I said, "What's so great on the bridge?"

"Scaring drunks." He grinned as we began to trot. "You can see 'em coming up from Main, driving like this." His hands wove back and forth. "The ghosts jump in front of the car and it goes right through the ghost, and the guy inside goes totally buggy. Did ya hear that one idiot? He nearly went right off the bridge." He laughed, a hoarse, high laugh. "Stupid drunks."

Pain lanced through me when he said, "Scaring drunks," but I wasn't about to show it. *Besides, why should I care anymore? My dad is dead.*

"Yeah, stupid drunks," I said, and laughed, just as meanly as he had.

———

"Where was Dad killed?"

My mother looked up from her coffee. "Good morning, Anna," she said brightly. "Please, sit down and have some breakfast. Here's some toast—"

"Where was Dad killed?" I demanded.

Next to Mom *he* sat, his eyes on the paper. He'd given up trying to talk to me a month before.

"You didn't want me to tell you the details," Mom said carefully, her eyes scanning back and forth across my face. "Are you sure you're ready for them now? You look like you aren't feeling well." She reached for my forehead and I stepped back. She pulled her hand down quickly.

"Just tell me where."

She looked over at *him*. He looked up, his brown eyes serious. "It happened out on the highway, Anna," he said. "Your father crossed the line into a logging truck. It was a dangerous curve—"

I walked out.

The rain started right after the dinner I didn't eat. I sat at my window and watched. First it pelted down, hissing and roaring. Then it tapered into soft drips. Then, slowly, it got stronger, until the drops between my window and the lamppost were like thin spears of icy white light.

At midnight, there was Ben, his hair hidden in the hood of a windbreaker. I grabbed my own windbreaker and pulled it on over my sweater. If he'd worn only a sweater, I would have to, too. No one would call me a sissy, afraid of a little wet. I was just as tough as any bad kid—and I cared even less.

216

When I landed, I had a coughing attack. After I caught my breath he said, "You sound sick. This will make it worse."

"Who cares?" I said. "*They* don't. Be glad to get rid of me. And since she already killed my dad and got away with it, why not me?"

"What?"

"My mother." I snarled the word so nastily it made me start coughing again. "Killed my dad."

"Geez!" Ben exclaimed, throwing up his hands. "Why is it some people have all the luck?"

"That my dad is dead?" I said, really angry now.

"No, no," he said quickly. "But here's you, sitting all period in math and English doing nothing, and nobody notices. Me, now, I look at one of them wrong, and it's back to detention. Then when I get home..." He gave one of those shrugs again. "So how'd she do it? And get away with it?"

"Dumped him," I said, a year's worth of bitterness making my voice shake. "He moved out and that disgusting idiot moved in with us. With *her*. Anyway, Dad started..." I hesitated, then said quickly, "She made him start drinking, but he wasn't some old drunk. So one night, something happened to his car..." I stopped and closed my mouth hard. I sure wasn't going to cry in front of some boy, and have him laugh at me.

"That's what I mean about luck," he said softly. "Why couldn't it be my father, and not yours? Hey, let's see if the ghosts come out in the rain."

The ghosts were there, clothes streaming and fluttering as if the rain were nothing but wind. They seemed delighted to see us.

Ben and his crowd went up to the bridge again. I didn't feel like doing much, so I mostly sat and watched Sarah and two other little ones playing some kind of game. Was it something kids had played a hundred years ago? I hugged my arms close, and as the silvery little-kid ghosts clapped soundlessly and hopped and twirled, I thought about how wonderful it would be to just hang out in a park for a hundred years, playing and playing. How lucky the ghosts were! The weather didn't have any effect on them; some of them were in summer clothes, but they just danced about like leaves in the wind, light and uncaring.

A movement by my leg made me look up, and I saw my little Sarah ghost. *She really does remind me of Sarah.* My sweet little cousin Sarah, whom I hadn't seen since Dad's funeral.

The little ghost looked into my face, her eyes and mouth sad. I reached out to pull her into my lap, like I used to with Sarah, but my hands went right through her. The air was so cold I shivered.

She stood there looking at me, sad and still and cold and not breathing, and I shivered again, without knowing why, except I knew that suddenly I missed Sarah horribly. She'd been kind of a little sister to me. Though I hadn't seen her for six months—hadn't really thought about her—I thought now, *What if she dies, just like this little girl? I'll never see her again.*

The screech of tires sounded like a scream this time.

I whirled around, saw from the glitter of lights through the rain that the car had turned completely around. A couple minutes later, there was Ben, wheezing with laughter.

"We better go," he said, still grinning as, around us, the ghosts laughed and danced. "Cops'll be here in a minute."

Just as we reached the edge of the park, red lights revolving up on the bridge made us turn and look. I saw the ghosts suddenly wink out, like candles being snuffed.

There was nothing to see but swings and slides and play equipment, with water running down it all in streams.

We started to run, but my chest hurt too much. I faltered, and Ben slowed again.

"That was fun," he said. "God, those drunks are stupid... I think I'd like to try faking 'em out. Just once. And if I end up playing forever in Neverland, who cares? Damn drunks," he said. And laughed again.

"Damn drunks," I said. But I didn't feel like laughing.

"Is Sarah there?"

"Who is this?"

I thought for a moment about lying. "Hi, Aunt Margaret. It's Anna."

"How are you doing, dear?" My aunt's voice was soft and careful.

"Okay. Is Sarah there?"

"Well, she's at her piano lesson. But we could call you back..."

I tried to think of something to say, but my throat closed up and my eyes burned.

"Anna? Anna?"

I hung up.

219

"I don't think you should do it," I said to Ben on the way to the park.

The air was bitter, with that funny smell—like a refrigerator's—that usually means snow is coming.

"Do what?"

"With the cars. Something might happen."

"They're just drunks," he said in his angry voice. "Drunks are mean, nasty, and they mess up everyone around them and don't give a damn."

I thought of the little ghost, and Sarah, and how the little ghost would never be warm again. Would never be hugged. But I couldn't say that out loud to a guy like Ben.

"What if the car goes over next time? And there's, like, a baby in the backseat? Or a grandmother? Or a kid like us?" *What if the drunk is someone like my dad?*

"That's the breaks," Ben said, still in that hard voice. "Drunks—"

"It's not the kid's choice to be there and die," I said. My voice got hard as well—better than crying.

"So the kid gets saved a whole lot of grief," he said, then he stopped, squinting at me. His face looked thinner than ever in the bleached light from a store window. It looked old. "What kid are you yakking about anyway, dork?"

"Anyone who didn't choose what was happening," I said. And because my voice went shaky—I didn't know why—I added, "Dork yourself. Stupid, selfish, pea-brained dork." And I ran ahead, as fast as I could, arriving at the park alone.

Keeping my back to the bridge, I pushed all the

swings high, and the ghost kids had a great time swinging up and jumping. They didn't fall like we would. They fluttered down, light and pale as ash after a fire.

When I got tired of that, I spun the carousel. A swarm of them jumped onto it, soundless except for the creak of cold steel.

Then my little Sarah ghost came up next to me, with her curly hair and pinafore and her long skirt with a ragged hem. She looked at me with her black eyes, blacker than the sky.

And I remembered that encyclopedia article. "Do you see the light?"

She blinked, looking right at me, so I said it again. By now I felt pretty stupid as I pointed at the nearest street lamp. "Do you see the light?"

She turned around in a slow circle. It meant she had heard me—the first time any of them had really made it clear they could hear us, and not just see us. It gave me a weird feeling.

She faced the other way for a time, then glanced back at me with a look of questioning. "Find the light," I said, and she turned around again.

I squinted in the direction she was facing, but all I saw were trees bounding the park, and beyond them, a row of stores.

But as I watched her, the expression on her face changed. Surprise, wonder. She looked up, unblinking, and this time I saw reflections in her eyes. Bright, silvery light—silver, gold, blue, all the colors, but brighter than stars.

It sent a prickly feeling through me, not fear—not quite—and I spun around, hoping I could see what she saw. Surrounding me were just the usual street lamps and store windows, their neon lights looking weaker than ever in the bone-cold darkness.

When I turned again, Sarah was walking slowly past me. She held her arms up, like someone was going to carry her, and again I spun, but I didn't see anyone there. And when I looked back, Sarah was gone.

The other ghosts went right on playing.

I was alone.

Alone, and my head ached, and my arms were cold. I didn't even look toward the bridge, but turned and ran home.

"Anna?"

I jumped off my bed. Too fast—I stopped, coughing hard.

"Anna?" My door opened, and Sarah peeked in.

She was real. Her face was flushed, her eyes brown and smiling. I hugged her hard, felt her warm cheek against mine, her solid little body in my arms. I could hear her heart beat, and mine, past my ragged breathing.

"Anna? Don't cry," she said. "Mom said if you want, I can come over and we can play. Or you can come to my house. Want to? I started collecting porcelain ponies, just like you." She grinned proudly. Her front two teeth were missing. "I have six now. Want to hear their names?"

I looked over at my collection, still lined up on the shelves that *he* had made. I hadn't even looked at them in months. "Sure," I said. "Tell me all about them."

———

At midnight, I was alone again. Ben hadn't come.

I couldn't sleep, even though I felt rotten. I kept thinking about Sarah's visit. How happy she was to see me. If I hadn't called, how long would I have gone without seeing her again? How careful all the adults were at dinner. Sarah didn't notice—she just gabbled away like always—but anytime I spoke, all the adults smiled and agreed, just like a row of robots. Like I was a bomb and might explode if they moved wrong. When Sarah and my aunt left, my mother thanked them for coming, and when the door was shut, *he* said, "Thank you for joining us this evening, Anna." Careful, polite. More of the bomb business.

But I felt like a bomb, I thought as I stared at the softly falling snow out my window. Like all my feelings about the divorce and Dad might blow up, and no one cared.

Except Sarah cared. And Aunt Margaret—otherwise why would she bring Sarah over, even though Mom divorced her brother?

My thoughts circled around and around, like the ghost kids on the carousel. Anger and happiness and sadness all fluttered and streamed, just like their clothes, leaving me feeling cold inside.

I thought about Ben again. Was he out there? *And if I end up playing forever in Neverland, who cares?* he'd said. Had he been playing alone in Neverland Park at night until the ghosts came?

I thought of those cars going right through the ghosts. They wouldn't go through Ben. Why hadn't I thought of that before, when I was yelling at him about drunks and cars and kids? That he was in danger, too?

Ben doesn't care, I thought. My thoughts whirled around the carousel again. *He doesn't care if anyone dies—including himself.*

The snow fell softly. It was cold and silent and scary in the park. Not even a ghost in sight. I toiled through the soft mounds of snow toward the bridge, coughing as I struggled up the embankment. Flickers of white seemed to dance between the trees, but I couldn't tell if they were ghosts, or snow, or tricks of my aching eyes.

When I got to the top, black spots smeared my vision. The ghosts were there, all of them, but my attention went straight to the skinny figure in the middle of the street, his thin hair and baggy sweatshirt and old, worn jeans outlined in the harsh beam of the oncoming headlights. His face pale as the ghosts'.

Gasping, I floundered toward him, kicking up snow in all directions.

He stood still and straight as the car wavered through the snowdrifts; the light veered away, then lit him again, then veered, and he was no more than a shadow in the dark.

Then the lights swung back, and the car was close. Closer.

And Ben didn't move.

All my spiraling feelings—Sarah, and the little dead girl ghost, and my dad who'd said he loved me but went away, and the stepdad who didn't say anything but made me things—it all blended into one thought, straight as those headlights aiming at Ben.

"No!" I yelled.

Ben's head jerked. For a moment I saw his face.

224

"Jump!" I screamed, with all my strength.

The sound mixed with the screech of car tires. Lights swung, the car roared away, and my smeary vision found the thin dark figure, limp as a rag doll, lying in the snow.

I flung myself down beside him. A dark stream came out of his mouth, looking black under the streetlight. Blood.

"Ben," I cried. "Don't die. Don't die."

"Anna." It came out like a groan. His eyes were open, black, the street lamp gleaming in them. And in my mind I heard his voice the other night, almost as pain filled as now, but then I'd heard the pain as anger. *Who cares? Who cares?*

"I was mad at you for not coming," I babbled. "But then I realized I missed you, and so here I am, I was going to walk *you* back."

"Better go...," he whispered. "Get in trouble."

I was about to say *I don't care* but suddenly I was sick of those words. I looked around. We were alone— even the ghosts were gone. "I'm getting help."

And as I ran to the corner phone, I realized I'd been dead wrong about Ben. He cared, but it seemed like no one else in his life cared about him.

I punched 911, reported the accident. Then I stared at the phone for a long second, knowing that if I called home, my secret life would be gone forever—that because my mother did care, she'd be very angry.

I stabbed at the numbers, reversing the charges.

"Anna?" She sounded terrified. "Anna, where are you?"

"At the bridge above Neverland Park. Mom, after

this is over you can ground me till I'm fifty, but now I gotta stay here. There's somebody who needs me."

I heard her take a deep, shaky breath. "I'm on my way."

I ran back to Ben.

"No light," he muttered, groping weakly with one hand. "Can't see ... Are the ghosts gone?"

I caught that hand and squeezed it. "No one here but us," I said, faking a laugh.

Ben was silent, his breathing ragged, which sent pain through me, sharp as ice shards. In the distance I heard sirens wailing, and I squeezed his hand again, harder.

"Unh," he groaned—a protest. But when I eased my grip, his fingers tightened on mine, just faintly.

I looked at his thin face, thinking about how I had chosen to surround myself in darkness, while he had actually been surrounded in darkness.

He squinted up at me. "They are gone. I can't see them."

"Maybe the ghosts found their light," I said. My eyes stung, my throat hurt, my nose was running. Footsteps clumped around us, flashlights glared in our faces. Hands reached, some to help him, some to push me away. But Ben's head turned toward me, so I gripped his hand and said, like making a promise, "Now we have to find our own."

KAREN JORDAN ALLEN

MRS. POMEROY

My Dear Classmates,

Sorry I can't make it to Ohio for our twenty-fifth re-union. But I decided to write this for the newsletter because somebody ought to tell about what happened in sixth grade. Some of you were there, but nobody really knows what Mrs. Pomeroy did to me. Me and Bobby Cross and who knows how many other boys.

I'm sure most of you re-member Bobby—he was

always getting into trouble. He used to swear in front of the teachers, and we all knew he stole our lunch money, too, though no one ever caught him. Nothing worked on him until Mrs. Pomeroy made him vanish.

The moment he disappeared, right out of his desk, I knew that what I'd heard at recess was true.

"Mrs. Pomeroy's a witch!" Jeff had said. "She does black magic and stuff."

"Don't be stupid. There's no such thing." That was Brian, always the skeptic.

"Then why do the sixth graders act so weird?" someone asked.

For five years we had watched the new sixth graders huddle in groups on the playground. They stopped talking whenever we younger kids went by. At first we thought they were talking about sex or something. Then once we heard someone whisper, "Mrs. Pomeroy." There was no way you could talk about sex and Mrs. Pomeroy at the same time. She was old and puffy, like a lumpy pillow, and she never raised her voice, but nobody in her sixth-grade classes ever disobeyed her, at least not that we knew.

So we all waited to get into sixth grade and find out what was so different about Mrs. Pomeroy.

It took just three days for Bobby to find out.

I sat a couple of seats behind him. I remember him digging through his desk—it was an awful rat's nest—and then he slammed the lid down and said a four-letter word right out loud.

Mrs. Pomeroy got all stiff and quiet. "Mr. Cross," she said, "that language is inappropriate in the classroom. You will apologize and go to the principal's office at once."

Bobby swore again. Stupid kid.

Mrs. Pomeroy shook her head and picked up a thin wooden ruler. "I don't like to do this," she said in her high, sweet voice, "but someone needs to teach you to be civil." The ruler came down on Bobby's hand with a little smack, and he was gone. Vanished. Not there.

Katie screamed and her friends grabbed her, afraid maybe that she'd be next. But Mrs. Pomeroy just looked at the clock and said, "No need for alarm, children. He'll be back in precisely five minutes. Now take out your reading workbooks and do page five. I need to close my eyes."

Of course we all took out our workbooks, and Mrs. Pomeroy closed her eyes without the least fear we'd misbehave, but we couldn't pay attention to anything except the clock. Sure enough, five minutes later Bobby appeared in his seat, eyes and mouth wide as if he'd just had a nightmare. He put his hands to his face and felt it all over, and then he started to cry.

"You may go to the rest room, Mr. Cross," said Mrs. Pomeroy. "But be back in two minutes. Not a second more."

"Yes, ma'am," he croaked. He was back in a minute and a half. The rest of the day he kept his head down and did whatever Mrs. Pomeroy told him to do. At recess he even stayed in to clean out his desk. On my way out I asked him what happened.

He shuddered. "I can't tell," he said in a wispy voice, "but it was horrible. *Horrible.*"

Bobby never did say what happened, but he didn't give Mrs. Pomeroy any more trouble, and nobody ever lost their lunch money again, either. After that, the rest of you were smart enough to mind Mrs. Pomeroy, too. I wish I had been.

I was pretty moody as a kid. Still am; you can ask my ex-wife. But I didn't mean to be bad, not really bad, not like Bobby. Sure, I got on teachers' nerves a couple of times. I think I tried to pass a note to Jill. And I hid Terry's gym shoes (yeah, Terry, that was me). Regular kid stuff.

But I admit it, the hat was a mistake. I hardly ever wore a hat. But I'd gotten this new baseball cap for my birthday, and I wanted to show it off at school, so I put it on at recess when we went out to play kickball. I had a lousy game. Got called out nearly every time I was up, and fell down and ripped the knee out of my pants. The girl I had a crush on then—you know who you are!—laughed and said I was a goof-up. It seems silly now, but at the time it felt tragic.

So when I went back to class I slumped in my chair and pulled my hat down and hoped Mrs. Pomeroy wouldn't notice me. Fat chance.

"Mr. Brown, please remove your hat. Gentlemen don't wear hats in school."

I pretended I didn't hear.

"Mr. Brown, remove your hat."

I sank lower and pulled the bill over my eyes. All I could see of Mrs. Pomeroy was her feet in those ugly open-toed shoes she wore, with her big toe sticking out of a hole in her stocking.

"Remove your hat at once, Mr. Brown!"

God help me, I said, "No."

She put her hand on my desk. It was wrinkly and purple and her veins stuck out like speed bumps. "You remember, don't you, what happens to young men who disobey me?"

I shrugged.

Her ruler stung my arm and everyone disappeared.

I was sitting alone in the classroom. All the desks were there, with books still on them, but I was the only person left. Then I saw Mrs. Pomeroy's hand on my desk. How could I have missed her?

I hadn't. The hand was connected to *me*. I went cold all over. *No, I thought, don't be a fool.* But when I flexed my fingers the hand moved.

I screamed. I screamed and screamed, and when I felt two hands on my shoulders I jumped, and screamed some more.

"*Shh,* Kip, it's all right." Mrs. Pomeroy, of course. Incredibly, she was smiling. "I do hate having to do this, but if you boys would just learn to mind, it wouldn't be necessary."

I was gasping and my heart pounded so much I could hardly hear her.

"Now, dear," she said, "touch your face."

I lifted those horrid purple hands and put them to my cheeks. The skin felt loose and powdery. Mrs. Pomeroy held up a little mirror. I steeled myself and looked into it, and I saw Mrs. Pomeroy. I had turned into Mrs. Pomeroy.

I wanted to throw up.

She patted my shoulder. "Listen, Kip. As long as you mind me, you'll be fine. You'll look and feel like yourself. But . . ." She lifted a finger. "If you disobey me or speak a word against me, you will look and feel like me until you correct your behavior. No one else will know—you will look like yourself to them—but *you* will see only my skin, my hands, and my face."

She leaned closer. Her breath smelled like old canned corn. "And if you ever tell anyone what happened here, you will never see yourself again. You will look like me forever. Is that clear?"

I nodded.

"Now sit here for a few minutes and think about it." She went back up to her desk. I put my head on my arms and sobbed. When I looked up, everyone was back in their desks and my hands were pudgy and normal. My hat was still on my head, too, so I quickly took it off and stuffed it into my desk.

"Thank you, Mr. Brown." Mrs. Pomeroy's voice turned my bones to pudding. I couldn't look at her. "You may go to the rest room," she said, "but be back in two minutes."

I managed to wobble out of the room. When I got to the bathroom and saw my own face in the mirror, I wanted to kiss my reflection. I was so pale my freckles stood out like inkblots, but I looked like me. What a relief.

But I needed to convince myself that it hadn't been a dream. So I gazed into the reflection of my own eyes and whispered, "I hate you, Mrs. Pomeroy."

A wave rippled across the glass. Mrs. Pomeroy's face stared back at me.

232

I shook and my teeth chattered. I cried out, "I'm sorry, I'm sorry!" The wrinkles smoothed and vanished. I splashed some water on my face and went back to class. But I never told any of you what happened. And I never gave Mrs. Pomeroy any trouble again.

That awful woman ruined my life.

How, you wonder? First, there are the nightmares. I dream that I turn into Mrs. Pomeroy, and no matter how much I plead or apologize I don't turn back into myself. I have a phobia of hats; a hat on my head makes me sick to my stomach, even in winter. And I can't bear to displease anyone. Before Mrs. Pomeroy, I wanted to be a lawyer or maybe go into politics. Now I'm just a third-rate government accountant. I couldn't even confront my own wife when I knew our marriage was in trouble, and by the time we talked, it was too late.

Was what I did so bad? It was only a stupid hat!

Kip leaned back and stared at the computer screen. His hands were trembling again. "She must be dead by now," he said to himself. "Dead, dead, dead." He started to cry again. Disgusting. He was forty-three and still crying about something that had happened in sixth grade. He needed serious help. But who would believe him?

He reached for a tissue.

His hand wrinkled and shrank up and his fingernails dropped off. Chunks of dry flesh fell away, leaving only bone.

He screamed.

It couldn't be happening, not now. He closed his eyes and concentrated on his breathing. In, out. In, out.

He opened his eyes and saw two skeletal hands. Trembling, he lifted one to his face and found empty holes where his eyes should have been. He couldn't bear to look at his body, but his bony hand clattered against bare ribs and his fingers caught on bits of fabric. He had turned into Mrs. Pomeroy. Dead Mrs. Pomeroy.

"I'm sorry!" he shrieked. "Mrs. Pomeroy, I'm sorry, I'm sorry! I didn't mean it, I won't tell, I promise!" He stabbed at the computer with his bony fingertips. It beeped. ARE YOU CERTAIN YOU WANT TO DELETE THIS DOCUMENT? "Yes, yes, yes," he muttered, clicking the mouse desperately.

Then he leaned his head on his monitor and sobbed.

Kip waited for the apology to take effect, for the flesh to return to his bones.

And he waited.

And waited.

And waited.

ABOUT THE AUTHORS

KAREN JORDAN ALLEN grew up in rural Indiana and now lives in Maine with her husband, Bill. She writes horror, fantasy, and science-fiction stories, plays the piano at her church, and teaches high school Spanish. There have been teachers in her family for five generations, but as far as she knows, none quite as *gifted* as Mrs. Pomeroy.

BRUCE COVILLE has written more than fifty books for children, among them *My Teacher Is an Alien*; *Jeremy Thatcher, Dragon Hatcher*; *Aliens Ate My Homework*; and a collection of short stories, *Oddly Enough*. He has worked as a grave digger, a toy maker, an air freight agent, an actor, and an elementary schoolteacher, as well as performing numerous other strange jobs—all of which prepared him for his current career as a full-time children's book writer.

DEBRA DOYLE and JAMES D. MACDONALD have been married since 1978 and writing together since 1986. Their books include the novels *Groogleman* and *Knight's Wyrd*, the middle-grade series *Circle of Magic*, the space opera series *Mageworlds*, and the Val Sherwood werewolf novels *Bad Blood*, *Hunters' Moon*, and *Judgment Night*. The *Bad Blood* series features the same characters who appear in the story in this book.

MARK A. GARLAND once played in rock bands and raced cars, but ten years ago he gave up the fast life to write science fiction. Since then he has published three novels, including *Dorella, Demon Blade,* and a Star Trek novel, *Ghost of a Chance*. He has also written a slew of short stories that have appeared in publications such as *Bruce Coville's Book of Nightmares*. He lives in upstate New York with his wife, his three children, and, of course, a cat.

NINA KIRIKI HOFFMAN is the sixth of seven children and grew up in Southern California, but she now resides in Eugene, Oregon, with four cats, a large TV, and a mannequin named Elvira. Her short stories frequently appear in anthologies and magazines such as *The Magazine of Fantasy and Science Fiction,* and she has published two novels: *The Thread That Binds the Bones* and *The Silent Strength of Stones*.

JOY OESTREICHER performed a wide assortment of jobs before becoming a full-time writer and mom. She has had stories in both *A Wizard's Dozen* and *A Starfarer's Dozen,* has edited the anthology *Air Fish* and a poetry magazine, and is presently at work on a novel about a troupe of child performers who travel the stars.

ALAN SMALE is from Bowie, Maryland, by way of an English childhood. He sings bass with an a cappella group and also with a less reputable bunch who perform at Renaissance festivals. He has published his fiction in *A Wizard's Dozen, Marion Zimmer Bradley's Fantasy Magazine, Terminal Fright,* and *Argonaut.* In his other life, he conducts research in X-ray astronomy at the NASA/Goddard Space Flight Center.

SHERWOOD SMITH began making books at the age of five, using paper towels, tape, and crayons. Since then she has gone on to write many books and short stories, including tales in *A Wizard's Dozen* and *A Starfarer's Dozen.* She is the author of the highly acclaimed young adult trilogy *Wren to the Rescue, Wren's Quest,* and *Wren's War,* and, with Dave Trowbridge, the science-fiction adventure series *Exordium.*

MARTHA SOUKUP has flown on airplanes dozens of times without anything *too* strange happening, but you never know. She has published several dozen stories in many anthologies and magazines, such as *Asimov's Science Fiction Magazine* and *Science Fiction Age,* and she won a Nebula Award for "A Defense of the Social Contracts." Her first story for younger readers appeared in *A Starfarer's Dozen;* a collection of her stories for adults has been published by DreamHaven Press.

NANCY SPRINGER's adult fantasy has been nominated for Hugo, Nebula, and World Fantasy awards, and her children's book honors include an IRA Children's Choice, an IRA Young Adults' Choice, the Joan Fassler Memorial Book Award, and, for *Toughing It* and *Looking for Jamie Bridger,* two Edgar Awards. She lives with her family in Dallastown, Pennsylvania.

STEVE RASNIC TEM has written more than two hundred stories that have been featured in books such as *Tales of the Great Turtle, It Came From the Drive-In,* and *David Copperfield's Tales of the Imagination.* He is also the editor of *High Fantastic,* an anthology featuring Colorado writers of fantasy, dark fantasy, and science fiction. He lives in Denver with his wife, the author Melanie Tem.

VIVIAN VANDE VELDE has written many strange and popular books, including *Tales from the Brothers Grimm and Sisters Weird, Companions of the Night, Dragon's Bait,* and *User Unfriendly.* Her stories and poems have appeared in a wide variety of magazines and books, including *Cricket, Asimov's Science Fiction Magazine,* and *A Wizard's Dozen.* She and her family live in Rochester, New York.

LAWRENCE WATT-EVANS began writing science fiction at age eight. He has written many popular novels, including the Ethshar fantasy series, which begins with *The Misenchanted Sword,* and the Three Worlds trilogy. His short stories have been nominated for several awards, and he won the Hugo for "Why I Left Harry's All-Night Hamburgers." He, his family, two cats, a parakeet, and a few thousand comic books all share a house in Maryland, near Washington, D.C.

JANE YOLEN has written more than 170 books, including *Passager, Hobby,* and *The Wild Hunt,* and the series of collections that begins with *Here There Be*

Dragons. She has won the World Fantasy Award and the Mythopoeic Society's Aslan Award, as well as several of the highest awards in children's literature. She and her husband divide their time between homes in Massachusetts and Scotland.